The Mad Disciples of Jacob Frank:
A Tale of the Demon Goddess

by

BARAK A. BASSMAN

TELEMACHUS PRESS

THE MAD DISCIPLES OF JACOB FRANK:
A TALE OF THE DEMON GODDESS

Cover designed by Telemachus Press, LLC

Cover art: ©Copyright iStock Photo/481079234/THEPALMER

Publishing services by Telemachus Press, LLC
7652 Sawmill Road
Suite 304
Dublin, Ohio 43016
http://www.telemachuspress.com

ISBN: 978-1-965121-00-9 (eBook)
ISBN: 978-1-956867-99-2 (Paperback)

Library of Congress Control Number: 2024916283

Version 2024.08.07

Table of Contents

The Mad Disciples of Jacob Frank:
A Tale of the Demon Goddess

I. An Old Man Learns of the Death of His Long-Departed Lord

ARYEH LIEB HAD long ago settled into a comfortably soft old age. Although in his younger days he had fearlessly tramped through miles of dark forests to supervise the harvest of His Lordship's timber, it had now been many years since he had passed his lumber business on to his two sons-in-law. These days, he mostly idled about his house in the little *shtetl* of R., although he did try to study each day for an hour or so in the *bet midrash*. He especially loved perusing the *Ein Yaakov*, that wondrous compilation of the miraculous tales and wise sayings of the holy sages of blessed memory, whose words sweetened his soul and eased the creaking arthritic pains in his bones.

However, one fine autumn day, in the middle of the morning, a splendid carriage pulled up in front of his house. The steward who managed the local nobleman's estate—the new steward, the younger one, Aryeh Lieb reminded himself—was seated inside. Aryeh Lieb, who was sitting on the porch, greeted him warmly, and said that neither of his sons-in-law was home at the moment—was there a message for one of them that he should pass on?

But the young steward smiled wryly and said: Aryeh Lieb, I have come here for you, not your sons-in-law. The old *Pan*—the one whom you knew so many years ago—has recently died in his palace in St. Petersburg. His son, the new *Pan*, has traveled here all the way from Russia to inspect his Polish estate. This young *Pan* is a real Russian—he is named Alexei, his mother is a Russian Countess, and he speaks barely any Polish and not a word of your Yiddish. I have to speak to him in French, which seems to be the only language we both know. And in his perfect French—did you know they speak French at the Czar's court?—he asked me to summon you to a meeting with him, as he has certain questions to put to you regarding his late father.

Aryeh Lieb felt a sudden chill in his bones. He had long tried—without success—to forget the days when the old *Pan* had held the countryside in terror. Still, he could not resist the summons from his lord. And so, Aryeh Lieb let his Miriam know that he was going to be away for the rest of the day, grabbed a bundle of food to eat on the journey, and sat down in the coach next to the young steward. A moment later they were off traveling briskly through the country roads, which cut through endless expanses of quietly rustling fields.

When they reached the nobleman's once grand manor house, the building looked to Aryeh Lieb like a tired old man sagging too low towards the ground. The paint was peeling, a step was broken on the porch, and through the open bay windows he could see that the formerly elegant and imposing furniture in the front parlor room was either gone or broken.

The young steward stammered out an apology for the state of the manor house—ever since His Lordship—the old one, the one who had just died—had moved to St. Petersburg, he had forbidden the use of any funds for the maintenance or improvement of this structure; all estate profits were instead diverted to his new palaces in Russia.

After they went inside and wound their way down a long, meandering hallway, they emerged into a small, square room in the back of the house. This room had bare white walls, a broad but simple desk, and four short, cushion-less wooden chairs. Seated in one of these uncomfortable looking chairs was a strikingly handsome and elegantly attired young man. Aryeh Lieb figured that this must be the new *Pan*, Alexei from Russia.

The steward greeted his young lord in some strange, musical language that Aryeh Lieb did not understand but assumed was French. After a couple of minutes of conversation between them in this tongue, the steward turned back to Aryeh Lieb and asked him, in Yiddish, to have a seat. Once they were all seated, the steward explained that he was going to translate between the young Count Alexei in French and Aryeh Lieb in Yiddish.

Then Count Alexei spoke: Aryeh Lieb, it is a pleasure to make your acquaintance. Even though you are a Jew who denies Christ Our Lord, you still faithfully and honorably served my father for many years. I have been told you are an honest man who never stole even a single ruble. My father hardly ever spoke of his years in Poland. Of course, I knew he hailed from these lands and that he was a Polish nobleman. But he preferred to dwell upon his days in Russia, and how splendid St. Petersburg was in the winter snow and how he had deftly maneuvered his way into the great balls thrown by the most famous Russian Princesses. He fell in love with my mother the moment he saw her enter one such grand ball. And—to the shock of all St. Petersburg—she too was soon enamored of him, a slave to her uncontrollable passion. Her family deemed his lineage to be beneath them—a Pole and not an especially impressive one, hardly worthy of her exalted blood—but she paid them no heed. He was rumored to have an estranged wife stashed away somewhere back in Poland, but he persuaded His Holiness the Patriarch of the Russian Orthodox Church that the supposed Polish marriage was a slander lodged against him by corrupt and ignorant Catholic heretics.

Thus, they were wed, and thus, I was born.

He was quite an extraordinary man, my father. Even as the years passed and age and drink and excessive luxury ravaged the other gallants of St. Petersburg society, my father not only remained handsome and vigorous, but actually seemed to grow stronger and more imposing with each passing season. Women swooned at his touch, and he had many mistresses, whose favors he drained to the dregs and whose hearts he discarded with contempt. And he loved to feast—he would devour many plates of delicacies in one sitting and down his vodka by the barrel, but his body was never the worse for the wear.

However, one day, my father suddenly became ill, even though I had never before heard him utter so much as a single cough or sneeze—his health and vigor having always been an impregnable fortress. Yet on this night, after dinner, as I was pursuing my studies—for I intended at that time to matriculate to the university in Konigsberg—he abruptly dropped his glass, let out a scream like a wild animal whose hide had just been penetrated by a hunter's bullet, and swooned headlong down onto the floor.

The doctor came the next morning and diagnosed fever and severe indigestion. He prescribed rest and a malodorous greenish powder to be mixed with water. But my father's condition did not improve with rest or medicine. To the contrary, his fever heightened, his screams grew hoarser, and he vomited up everything he tried to eat.

After three days of these agonies, he died.

I was deeply suspicious of the circumstances of his death, which struck me as far from natural. As he had been a man in perfect health before being felled by this sudden and mysterious illness, I worried that he had been poisoned. Commencing upon my own investigation of his papers and effects, I made certain significant and unsettling discoveries. However, I do not wish to share these details with you, Aryeh Lieb—at least not yet.

For now, I shall get to the point. You must be wondering why I have summoned you. As you have never set foot in St. Petersburg, you must be thinking that you cannot have any connection to my father's death. You have certainly not spoken to him for many years, probably decades.

Yet my investigations led me back to the time when my father lived here in Poland, on this estate and in this house. In particular, I believe his possible murder to be closely linked to his past intrigues in Poland with an individual named Pawel. However, no one seems to be acquainted with the Pawel who knew my father. And when I wrote to my steward for this estate—the gentleman sitting here and translating for us—he likewise knew nothing of any Pawel.

Puzzling over this mystery, I examined my father's papers again. Upon this second, closer inspection, I discerned certain oblique references to an Aryeh Lieb on the Polish estate, a Jewish timber merchant who was somehow entangled in the affairs of my father and Pawel. This time, my faithful steward knew exactly of whom I wrote. I decided to make haste to visit this estate so I could question you myself in person (and also because this estate has been long neglected and is overdue for a proper inspection).

Now, tell me, Aryeh Lieb, are you, or were you, acquainted with a gentleman named Pawel? And if so, what was the nature of his relations with my father?

Aryeh Lieb was not pleased to hear the name Pawel spoken again in that manor house after so many years. Pawel—that miserable heretic, follower of the false Messiah and charlatan Jacob Frank, an embarrassment to the Jewish people—may his worthless corpse be a feast for the worms and the maggots. Still, he reflected silently to himself: This young man is now lord and master of these lands. But he knows none of us who live here—and certainly not my sons-in-law whose livelihoods depend upon leasing his timber rights. If I anger him, who knows what he might do to them in response? And anyway, he says he wants to know the truth about his dead father, so fine, let him hear what kind of a man his father was.

Aryeh Lieb then said aloud that he had known Pawel and he would tell all he could remember about him and the old *Pan*.

II. A Midnight Summons

ARYEH LEIB NOW began his tale: Your Honor, I met Pawel many years ago, when I was dragged from my bed in the middle of the night. I had been sleeping soundly and dreaming happy dreams, when suddenly my fat old maidservant shook me so hard that I nearly fell on the floor.

When I asked her what she thought she was doing, she said: There is a man downstairs with a big carriage and a driver. He says the *Pan* wants to see you, right now. You are to come downstairs and go with him to His Lordship. That is what the man said.

I asked her: Who is this man? What is his name?

But she only shrugged and yawned and walked off.

I considered whether I should go back to bed and deal with whatever this was the next morning—after all, in our little *shtetl* of R., nothing terribly important ever happened, and I could not imagine what could possibly be so urgent that a man had to be driven from his warm bed in the middle of the night.

But then I recalled that the *Pan* had only recently returned to his estate in the country. In those days, your father usually preferred to reside in Warsaw. Sometimes he would also travel, always to some famous city: Vienna, Budapest, Paris, Venice, Rome, Naples, even Constantinople once.

I had no idea why the *Pan* had suddenly abandoned Warsaw for the countryside. And now His Lordship wanted to speak to me of all people in the middle of the night. What choice did I have in the end but to obey the *Pan*'s mad whims and put my faith in the Holy One, Blessed be He, to see me through this ordeal?

And so, I quickly dressed, left a brief note for my wife should I not be back by sunrise, and went downstairs, where I found the old steward waiting in my kitchen. He said to me: I have been ordered to bring you to the manor house. Come Aryeh Leib, the carriage is outside.

I followed him outside and into the coach. I was trembling with terror during that whole carriage ride. I remember it was so dark that night that you could not see anything out the carriage windows—there must have been thick clouds covering the moon and the stars—but I still heard the wolves howling. I wondered what could be awaiting me at the manor house—Did His Lordship think that I had stolen from him? Was I going to be thrown into a cell, and beaten and starved until I confessed to some made up crime?

To ease my worries, I tried to get the steward to tell me more about what was happening and why I was being dragged out of my bed at such a crazy hour. I asked him: What could possibly be so urgent that it could not wait until after my prayers tomorrow morning?

The steward groaned and sighed, and then he said to me: I do not fully understand it myself. The *Pan*'s heart is bitter because this Katerina—a Russian lady whose father gambled away her family's estates, and who now trades on her beauty among the rich lords and merchants in Warsaw, a filthy whore with no respect for God or the sanctity of marriage—spurned him. He fell at her feet amidst a gathering of nobles in the salon of a famous countess in Warsaw, and begged for her to take him back. But in reply she only mocked his newly sprouting wrinkles and thinning hair. He was laughed at and driven away in shame. I would have hoped that such a humiliation would spur him to atone for his sins and reconcile with his estranged wife, who still resides upon her father's estate.

But instead, he fell in with this man, this stranger—how can I describe him? His parents were Jews who accepted baptism. Yet their baptism was insincere. They were followers of some mad Jewish sorcerer or alchemist who ordered his disciples to convert in order to escape persecution by the rabbis. But after converting, he was exposed to the Church authorities as an unrepentant heretic. The Church imprisoned him for many years in the fortress in Czestochowa but eventually someone let him out— the Russians maybe. Well, this stranger whom the *Pan* met was raised in this heretic sorcerer's sect and he told the *Pan* that he had learned powerful, secret wisdom from the sect about goddesses and immortality and boundless wealth.

The *Pan* now passes his days in hushed and passionate conversations with this stranger. Until suddenly, the two of them demanded to see you tonight, without delay. You ask why they want to see you now, at this late hour? Well, my honest response is: I don't know. Who can say what ideas go through the heads of madmen?

III. The Lord in His Manor

AFTER A WHILE, between the heavy darkness and the steady rhythm of the wheels, I drifted off to sleep. The steward woke me again when the carriage had come to a halt. After I once more rubbed the sleep from my eyes, I saw we were in front of the *Pan*'s manor house—the same house where we are sitting right now.

I followed the steward inside. There were no servants to greet us—they all must have been asleep—and we went from the dark vestibule into a dark hallway. Then the steward pushed open a door and my eyes were blinded by a painfully bright light. We had entered the *Pan*'s parlor room. I had rarely set foot in this room before, as usually when I came to the manor house, I met with the steward in his cramped study in the back where the account books were kept.

To tell the truth, this parlor room frightened me a bit. It reminded me of the tales that my *bubbe*, of blessed memory, used to tell me when I was a little boy—tales about mysterious mansions in the forest inhabited by demons, full of dazzling, unearthly delights and pleasures. But if you should be so foolish as to taste the food or kiss the serving girl, then your soul was lost and you were trapped there forever, a prisoner for eternity.

Standing next to the marble fireplace were the *Pan* and a stranger. The *Pan* looked like a man whose fortunes had fallen: His once mighty head of thick hair had thinned and receded, and there were lines on his brow and bags under his eyes. And for his part, the stranger was also not that impressive a sight. He was tall and narrow, like an overgrown blade of grass, swaying—or twitching—back and forth. While he looked like a Jew, his face was clean-shaven, his head was bare, and he had no *payes* or *tzitzit*. He was dressed like a German merchant, although his clothes fit him poorly.

The steward spoke first: My Lord, your leaseholder, Aryeh Lieb, the Jew, is here in answer to your summons.

The *Pan* turned to me, grinning wildly like a drunkard or a lunatic, and said: My dear Aryeh Lieb, welcome! Permit me to introduce you to my new companion, Pawel (he pointed to the stranger), who has graciously agreed to tear himself away from the delights of Warsaw society in order to keep me company in the country.

I tried to imagine this *shlemiel* Pawel dancing with some elegant countess at a ball in Warsaw and I was forced to stifle my laughter. But at least the ridiculous image in my mind calmed my nerves.

The *Pan* continued: You may be wondering why I have chosen to visit this estate again after so prolonged a period of absence. I have grown weary of the snares and deceits of the false ladies of Warsaw and the other great capitals of Europe. But not only that— after all, why would I drag you out of your bed in the middle of the night just to tell you of my sorrows in love? And what would some greasy little *Zhyd* like you know about love? No, I have brought you here tonight because of my dear new friend, Pawel. At a time when my heart was sinking fast in the fetid swamp of Warsaw society, I met Pawel one afternoon in a café I often to frequented. Even though he was a stranger at the time, he sat down right across from me at my table without so much as asking my leave. I once would have repaid such an insult with a good thrashing with the backside of my sword. But just then I was so melancholy that I appreciated any sympathetic companionship.

Pardon my interruption, Pawel said to me, but I must speak to you urgently about a matter of the utmost importance—a matter of life and death—a matter of immortality and eternal youth.

Although I thought him likely mad, I decided to hear what he had to say, as at least it would be a brief distraction from my own troubles. And what he had to say did indeed sound mad: He had made a pilgrimage to the shrine of the Black Madonna in Czestochowa and had been blessed there with terrifying and wondrous visions. Pawel had been reared in the teachings of some Jewish sorcerer or alchemist—for Pawel's family are Jews like you, or they were before their baptism—that there is a Holy Maiden, a goddess of some kind, who can bestow the gifts of immortality, eternal youth and beauty, and boundless wealth. The wild visions that Pawel received from the Black Madonna apparently confirmed the truth of these teachings for him.

After conducting further research in the library of the Jasna Gora monastery in Czestochowa, Pawel concluded that the means for reaching this Holy Maiden and harnessing her power is located somewhere within my estate. He had read in an old dusty Latin manuscript that, hundreds of years ago, there had lived a beautiful noble lady who was a woman of ferocious appetites—no amount of wine or lovers could ever satisfy her—and who was able, with her touch, to make her favorites as young and beautiful as she wished and to shower them with wealth that seemed to materialize out of the air. Pawel was convinced that this noblewoman had been the incarnation of his Holy Maiden and, moreover, that she had lived on the lands that now comprise my estate, quite close to where we are standing now, centuries later.

Unfortunately for her, certain narrow-minded religious fanatics believed her miraculous powers had come from Satan and they had her put to death. Nevertheless, her devoted followers cut the head off of her corpse and placed it inside some sort of fantastical box. They decorated this box with bizarre symbols and placed it on the altar of an abandoned chapel in the forest where they would pray to her in secret. Still, their secrecy was not quite absolute, and rumors soon spread of the miracles that were wrought by this lady's decapitated head—a head which, so the manuscript reported, never decomposed and appeared so fresh that it seemed still to be alive. Peasants and nobles, men and women, and even some priests traveled to the forest chapel in the middle of the night to beseech this strange relic to cure an illness or restore love or good fortune. According to the gossip of the countryside, these prayers were never uttered in vain.

Alas, word of these rites eventually reached the ears of the Church, which pronounced a harsh judgment upon the congregation of the little chapel in the woods: Heretics and witches, whose miraculous deeds could only be explained as the rotten fruit of infernal pacts with the Devil. The Bishop dispatched a troop of knights to ambush the worshippers at night and burn down their chapel with all of them locked inside of it.

When the dawn arose, and the chapel had been reduced to a charred ruin strewn with ashes and bones, one young knight, a man of deep faith who had not hesitated to smite the heretics, spied an elegant box sitting atop the rubble. Incredibly, the box was not singed or damaged, as if the flames had been careful to avoid it.

When the knight approached this box, the lid flipped open of its own accord, revealing inside the severed head of the most beautiful woman he had ever seen. Her eyes opened and she said something to the knight, but the monk who authored the chronicle had unfortunately received no reliable report of her exact words. Then the box closed—again of its own accord—and burrowed itself deep into the ground. Since that day, no one has seen this box or the magical decapitated head inside of it. For his part, the pious knight shortly thereafter lost his wits and spent his few remaining days in bed with a burning fever and babbling nonsensically.

Pawel assured me that the box must still exist and, what was more, he was certain it was buried somewhere on my estate. If we could find the box and wield its power, he and I would enjoy unending youth and beauty and wealth untold. He begged to be taken to my estate so he could begin his search immediately.

After Pawel was finished, I burst out laughing and told him to get out of my sight and bother someone else with his mad schemes. When he would not budge from his chair, I ordered my coachman, who was with me, to forcibly remove Pawel from the café, which he did—rather roughly, I am ashamed to admit, in light of our current warm relations.

Once Pawel was gone, I returned to my melancholy brooding over the cruelty and treachery of the cold-hearted coquettes of Warsaw.

However, over the next few days, wherever I went, I observed Pawel following me in the distance. I ducked in and out of alleyways and churches and cafes to avoid him, but somehow, he would always turn up again. If I visited an old friend, for an evening of cards and brandy, he would be loitering about that friend's door when I departed for the night.

Finally, one afternoon, I ordered my coachman to grab Pawel off the street and shove him into the back of my carriage. Once he was apprehended and seated next to me, I asked him why he would not leave me alone.

He said to me: The sacred box, the enchanted relic of the Holy Maiden, is buried on your estate. You must permit me to retrieve it.

To which I replied, in a firm and perhaps somewhat rude tone: Sir, you must realize that you sound like a madman. Why should I believe you when you say there is a magic box with some kind of talismanic witch's relic buried on my estate?? If such a marvel actually existed on my ancestral lands, I would have surely heard of it long ago.

Pawel breathed heavily and looked down at his feet for quite some time without speaking a word in reply. Eventually, though, he spoke up again: With your leave, I would like to depart now and return to my lodgings. I will attempt to reach the Holy Maiden through the veil that separates her world from ours. I have had visions of her before, I know where she is—but still, she does not always answer me. If she gives you a sign—and you will know if it happens—then I beg you to call upon me at my apartment. And he gave me his address scrawled out on a slip of paper.

And with that, I ordered the driver to halt, and Pawel exited the carriage.

The next few days were uneventful. Pawel ceased to follow me around Warsaw. Nor did I receive any supernatural signs or wonders. One evening, though, when I was reclining in my most comfortable chair with a glass of excellent sherry (the gift of a dear friend just returned from a visit to London), my valet abruptly burst into the room and announced that the Lady Such-and-Such was downstairs and insisted on speaking to me immediately.

I shivered with both a tingling delight and a melancholy nostalgia when I heard that name. For in my youth, long before I married and then cast aside my miserable shrew of a wife, this Lady had been my first lover and tutor in the affairs of the heart. I could not imagine why she would seek me out now after all these years, and especially on some urgent errand. Still, I was curious to see her. Perhaps the extinguished flame could be kindled once more? So, I told my valet to admit her and bring her to me in the parlor.

I nearly fainted from shock when I saw her. While I recalled loving a maiden with rosy cheeks and thick yellow curls and perfectly rounded shoulders, I now beheld a decrepit old hag, her face dried out and twisted into wrinkles and folds, her hair thin and white, and her back bent in obvious pain. I did not understand— it had not been that many years—perhaps ten, twelve at the most? Had she been the victim of some loathsome pox? But what disease could turn a ravishing young woman into a stooped crone in such a short amount of time?

She cast her eyes upon the floor and would not look at me. I heard her stifle more than one tear. For a long time, she sat there in silence, sniffling, trembling. I was not sure what to do or say, so I sat there in silence, as well, agog at this hideous marvel.

Finally, she spoke to me, but in such a thin, rasping voice that I was compelled to lean in closely to hear her words. This is the tale she told: Until three days ago, her life had been proceeding as it always had—lovers, balls, and salons in which her beauty and wit both sparkled, punctuated by an occasional quiet evening relaxing on a couch with a novel in French or English. She had been reading Voltaire—*Candide* and *Zadig*. Not that I suppose you have the faintest clue what I am talking about, Aryeh Lieb. Have you ever read anything that wasn't written by some dead rabbi?

But then, three days ago, while her servants were arranging her hair and applying powder and rouge to her face, in the mirror directly in front of her, she suddenly saw the door to the room open and a tall, strikingly beautiful woman entered, although this lady was dressed bizarrely, like a damsel from the Middle Ages—like an overdone illustration from an old knightly romance. However, she did not hear the door open or hear the sound of footsteps. Nor did her servants seem to notice that anyone else had entered the room. And because of their labors on her hair, she had to face rigidly forward, eyes toward the mirror, and could not turn her head around to survey the rest of the room.

In the mirror's reflection, the stranger was walking closer to her, until she stood right behind the lady's back. Then the stranger's face darkened into a grimace, and she opened her mouth wide as if she was screaming, although my former mistress heard not a sound. Still, the sight so terrified her that she threw the mirror to the ground, shattering it into pieces. She jumped up and shoved her servants away so she could confront the intruder, but when she looked behind her and around the room, no one was there.

After catching her breath, she reasoned that she must have hallucinated the whole strange episode—perhaps a poisonous mushroom or herb had been snuck onto her dinner plate? And thus, there was no genuine danger outside of her own fervid imagination. With her nerves now at ease again, she instructed her servants to finish their work. Once they were done, she quickly departed for a rendezvous with her latest lover, a handsome Prussian diplomat with a fine and manly fencing scar across his left cheek.

But when she arrived at the residence of the Prussian, and smuggled herself into his bedroom through a discreet back entrance, she found, to her shock, that he was unwilling to receive her favors. As soon as his eyes fell upon her face, his passion seemed to have evaporated into the air. He begged her forgiveness, but said she had to leave at once as he had just come down with a terrible headache.

She stormed off, indignant, outraged even. *She* was the one who developed sudden headaches when she grew tired of her lovers. Indeed, earlier that day, he had sent her two notes, feverishly scribbled in his own hand, pleading desperately for her to visit him that evening. So, what could have happened?

After returning to her apartments, she looked at herself again in the mirror. She discovered that she had somehow aged many years in the blink of an eye, so that her face had grown bloated and slack like a woman well into her plump middle age. Her hair, also, seemed shorter and thinner. And then, at the edge of the mirror's reflection, she saw *her* again—the strange lady in the medieval gown from the other mirror that she had shattered earlier that evening. The stranger now appeared in this new mirror's reflection to be standing in a corner of the room, arms folded, smirking and snickering.

But when my former mistress turned her head to have a look, once again there was no one else in the room.

Over the course of the next two days, she swiftly declined into pitiful old age. Terrified of beholding either her own suddenly ugly countenance or the mysterious stranger, she ordered every mirror in the house to be covered. She refused to go out and let it be known that she was confined to her bed with a fever.

She passed the time curled up in a chair, sobbing, napping, and then waking only to sob even more. She thought of sending for her doctor, but how could she ever explain what had happened? He would assume that the woman talking to him was not my former mistress, but rather some crazy old woman, perhaps a distant relation, and that the real lady of the house had absconded with her latest lover to a palazzo in Italy (which, truth be told, she had done many times before).

Every limb in her newly decrepit flesh was stiff as iron and burned with pain when she tried to move it. She tried to drink a strong draught of vodka to dull the pain but her trembling hands could not hold the glass. She cursed her fate and prayed for a quick death.

And then she fell asleep again. In her dream, she was standing on a wide balcony in a palace by the sea. In front of her was a tall mirror in a gilded frame. Out of this mirror stepped the same mysterious lady in medieval dress. This time, the stranger spoke to her: If you wish to have your beauty restored, then you must go to your former lover—and she named me—and tell him that the Holy Maiden can give the gifts of eternal youth and beauty and can take them away. The wrinkles in your face and the cracks in your bones are the signs by which he is to know me. Deliver this message and your lovely hair and young, supple skin will be restored to you.

When she awoke, she ordered her servants to take her to my residence that very instant.

I considered whether to believe this tale. Had Pawel's Holy Maiden sent me a sign and a wonder, a proof of her potency? Or was this all a cunning ruse? Perhaps Pawel had paid some old woman to dupe me. This would not be the first time that a scheming adventurer had sought to trick a rich nobleman into parting with his money to protect against a supposed supernatural menace that was in truth merely a set of clever deceptions. I have certainly heard many tales told of the intrigues of Cagliostro and Casanova.

Nevertheless, the old woman sitting in my parlor seemed to be genuinely suffering. It would have been cruel to have accused her of being a fraud. Maybe she had only gone along with this farce because she was a destitute widow in need of a few coins for bread? So, I thanked her graciously for delivering her message, and she promptly excused herself and left.

I gave the matter no further thought for the next several days. But then one evening, at a card game hosted by a gentleman whom I distantly knew, I saw my first love standing in a corner just as I had remembered her in all her alluring beauty, slowly sipping her wine and casting her smiles into the crowd of eager, bobbing men. While I was certain the old woman had been a fraud, my encounter with her had left me curious to know how my former mistress was faring, and so I decided to strike up a conversation with her.

But when I approached, she instantly burst into tears and embraced me tenderly. She thanked me profusely for saving her life and swore I had won her eternal favor and gratitude.

I asked her to explain what exactly it was that I had done.

And she replied: But how can you not remember? That demon witch, whom I saw in the mirrors, had rendered me old and decrepit and would have certainly killed me. But once I had unburdened my heart to you, my youth and health and beauty were restored to me, as if I had never been ill. Again, you have my eternal gratitude.

Now I realized that the old woman had been no trick—for my former mistress was too grand and proud a noblewoman to dabble in the intrigues of some lowborn baptized Jew like Pawel. I had truly received a wonder and a sign from Pawel's Holy Maiden. When I returned to my apartments later that evening, I rummaged through my desk drawers until I found the slip of paper with Pawel's address upon it. The next morning, I called upon him in his modest but respectable rooms. I told him everything that had transpired. We spoke for several hours that day, and he taught me many extraordinary secrets that had been revealed by the apostate Jew sorcerer Jacob Frank, the heretic whose doctrines Pawel and his family followed. I agreed with Pawel that we must find the enchanted box buried beneath the woods in my lands—that enchanted box containing the decapitated head of the noble lady who had once been the incarnation of the Holy Maiden in our world.

Hence, for the first time in many years, I resolved to return to this estate. Upon our arrival, I summoned my steward—who is supposed to be managing my affairs here—and interrogated him closely on the various landmarks in the forest in order to determine the probable location of the remains of the burnt down chapel.

But it was soon obvious that the steward had rarely, if ever, set foot in my woods. Who then was looking after this part of my estate? And then I remembered you, Aryeh Leib. You have the leasehold on the timber rights, which you have managed quite well—there were many noblemen in Warsaw who envied how much ready money was always at my disposal.

Once I had recalled that it is you, Aryeh Leib, who is truly master of my woods, I wasted no time in summoning you even though it was the dead of night. There is no task more urgent than finding this enchanted box and tapping into the power of the Holy Maiden. I can already feel my flesh begin to decay. I was once the handsomest man in Warsaw. At my approach, pretty maidens would blush and stare and giggle nervously. But now, as my more recent and unfortunate love affairs have demonstrated only too clearly, I have lost my power over the fairer sex. I am just another ageing fool, vain and corpulent and ugly, whom they beguile for amusement or profit, and then discard when the mood suits them. My past was a triumph, but in my future, I foresee defeat and ruin.

Yet the Holy Maiden can end my suffering—she can restore my youth and vigor and beauty.

I must find her magic box.

Now, my dear Aryeh Lieb, tell me, in your many days and nights tramping about my forest, have you come across the ruins of a chapel? Or perhaps an unusually large mound of dirt in a clearing?

IV. Pawel's Tale

AND THAT, YOUR Honor, is what I remember hearing from your father's lips on that crazy night. I was sure he had gone mad. But on the other hand, If I said or did anything to upset His Lordship, who knew what he might do.

I decided to delay answering him until after I had a chance to rest and clear my mind. So, I said to the old *Pan*: Your Honor, please forgive me. Although you have spoken at great length, and with much wisdom, I fear that, in my exhausted state, my memories of the forest paths are concealed inside a thick fog. Please permit me to sleep somewhere—anyplace will do—and after I am rested my thoughts will be clearer.

Much to my relief, the *Pan* nodded in agreement. At his signal, the steward woke a servant, who then made up a bed for me, where I lay down and fell instantly into a deep dreamless sleep.

The next morning, I told the *Pan* that I recalled seeing a tall mound in a clearing in the forest that could contain the buried ruins he was looking for. His Lordship was happy to hear this, and he ordered a wagon to be hitched and about a quarter of an hour later Pawel and I were riding into the woods together.

From everything His Lordship had said about him the night before, I was wary of this Pawel. He had acquired a great influence over the *Pan*—and this influence was not, to my thinking, good for the Jews in our *shtetl*. Pawel was a follower of the charlatan and criminal Jacob Frank—a wretched, evil man who had once persuaded a Bishop to seize copies of our holiest books and burn them. That such a person was now a close companion to our lord, upon whose protection we depended, was a danger I would need to warn our rabbi and community elders about. And to understand better the threat we faced, I wanted to know more about Pawel—who he was and what he thought, as opposed to what the *Pan* said he thought.

So, as we were riding into the forest together in the back of the wagon, I asked Pawel if he could explain more to me about his Holy Maiden. Pawel did not need much encouraging, and he immediately launched into the tale of his life—I imagine he never passed up an opportunity to regale a willing listener with his crazy ideas—you also must know the type, right? As best I recall, here is what he told me:

Reb Aryeh Lieb, it will be difficult for you to hear what I must tell you, as you have been told so many lies. But I implore you, listen closely to my words and do not blindly trust that everything you have been told by your rabbis is true. For they are in league with the dark forces that oppress you and me and every other man who walks this earth bound in our chains. They are the living letters of the law that breeds death, disease, and misery.

My parents were both born Jews in the Kingdom of Poland. For many generations, their families had, in defiance of rabbinical bans and decrees and persecutions, secretly maintained their faith in the Lord Messiah Sabbatai Zevi. I see from your face that you have soaked up the slanders that have been spread against him. You think Sabbatai Zevi was a liar and a fraud, right? That his conversion to Islam showed the falsity of his claim to be the Redeemer? You think you understand these matters, but you do not.

After the holy prophet, may his memory be blessed, Nathan of Gaza—a great scholar of the *kabbalah* in the Land of Israel—had revealed that Sabbatai Zevi was the Messiah, hundreds of Jews, thousands of Jews, young and old, men and women, rich and poor, fell down in the middle of the streets in every city and town, foaming at the mouth, losing consciousness, their limbs flailing wildly about. And when they came to again, they all reported that angels and heavenly voices had proclaimed that Sabbatai Zevi was the Messiah.

And as the age of the Messiah had now begun, the old prohibitions became obsolete. With the arrival of the Redemption, we could return to life as it had existed in the Garden of Eden, before Adam's sin and fall, when there were no distinctions between the prohibited and the permitted. In the Garden of Eden, there was no old age, no sickness, and no death. Thus, Sabbatai Zevi ushered in the new age by abolishing the fast days and casting aside the shackles of a law, the Torah, which was meant only for a fallen, unredeemed world.

Nevertheless, much of the world stubbornly clung to its unredeemed state. There had to be a part of his mission that Sabbatai Zevi was failing to fulfill. But what was it? He had won over almost all the Jews and none in Israel dared oppose him openly. As a Jew, he had thought that was all that would be necessary. But then he grasped a deeper, harsher truth: The forces of evil, of what he, as a good Jewish Kabbalist, called the *kelipot*, were entrenched not merely among the Jews but also the nations of the world. As long as he remained a Jew, he could not reach these demons buried deeply within the Gentile world and free the holy sparks of divine light that they had trapped and imprisoned.

And so, Sabbatai Zevi permitted himself to be seized and arrested by the Sultan of Turkey. When the Sultan offered him the choice of conversion to Islam or death, he donned the turban without hesitation. Now, as a Muslim, he could set to work upon the next stage of the Redemption as he had left the Jewish world for the Gentile one.

But the mass of blind fools among the Jews did not understand the terrible spiritual war that Sabbatai Zevi was waging against the *kelipot*. Instead, his enemies—those rabbis still in thrall to their Torah with its labyrinth of prohibitions and restrictions—saw their opportunity and denounced him as a fraud because he had converted to Islam. They said the Messiah must be a Jew who will restore Israel to worldly splendor and might, a new King David who will ascend the Jewish throne in Jerusalem. The Jews who had once flocked to Sabbatai Zevi as their Redeemer were now easily seduced by their rabbis' lies.

Yet there was a holy remnant who maintained their faith in Sabbatai Zevi. Heeding the wise words of mighty sages like Nathan of Gaza and Abraham Miguel Cardoso, they grasped the true, occulted meaning of Sabbatai Zevi's conversion to Islam. My forefathers were among this remnant. Theirs was a bitter lot, as the believers in Sabbatai Zevi were persecuted all across Europe. My grandparents and great-grandparents were repeatedly forced to flee from their homes and always had to conceal their sacred manuscripts setting forth the Messiah's teachings.

But they were steadfast in their faith that Sabbatai Zevi's soul would return one day, incarnated in a new body, to complete his work. And behind the veil of their tightly drawn, dark, thick curtains, they worshipped with a fervor, with an ecstasy and a delight, that a Jew like you Aryeh Lieb, accustomed to your drab and mechanical devotions, cannot imagine.

And then it came to pass one day that my parents heard the tidings for which all the believers had waited so long: Sabbatai Zevi's soul had returned to this lowly world, incarnated in a new body—as a Turkish Jew named Jacob Frank. My parents traveled to him in the *shtetl* of Lanckorona, where he had established a congregation, and pledged themselves to him and his teachings. They worshipped with him and his other disciples in secret, breaking the chains of the prohibitions of the Torah and giving themselves up to the freedom and pleasure that are the portion of all men in the age of the Messiah.

But once again, the wicked persecutors, the servants of darkness and oppression, came for them. My parents and the other members of Jacob Frank's Holy Company of Brothers and Sisters were arrested and imprisoned. The scheming little rabbis begged the lords of the Catholic Church to burn the heretics alive. But even though my parents may have quaked in terror, their faith never faltered.

And that faith was rewarded: The Bishop set them free and even arranged for them to publicly debate their doctrines against the rabbis. But the rabbis' hearts remained hardened, and they continued to plot against the believers. Jacob Frank now grasped, as Sabbatai Zevi had grasped before him, that the Messiah could not complete his sacred mission if he remained a Jew. He thus led his followers, including my parents, to the baptismal font and they all became Christians.

But the Church soon learned that Jacob Frank did not genuinely believe in their faith and was instead continuing to pursue his mission as the Messiah. In punishment for his heresies, the Church imprisoned him in the fortress at Czestochowa.

Yet it was at Czestochowa that Jacob Frank was to learn the great truths that could deliver his believers from their bondage to the laws and prohibitions of this fallen world. The wonder of Czestochowa is the painting of the Black Madonna that hangs in the chapel of the Jasna Gora monastery. Jacob Frank would watch as swarming crowds of pilgrims dropped to their knees before her and, tears rushing down their cheeks, begged the Madonna for her aid and blessing.

It was then that Jacob Frank understood that the Christian Madonna and the Jewish *Shekhinah* are one and the same. Or rather that they are both reflections, or perhaps silhouettes, of the same underlying truth: That there is a Holy Maiden, a *Matronita*, who is the source of abundance—the source of the eternal youth and beauty and health and endless riches that were promised to man in the Garden of Eden. But she is hidden from us—she is exiled from us. We can only glimpse aspects of her as if we were watching her from behind a curtain. But if we can find a path to reach her, then she will grant us her gifts.

Who exiled her? Our lord and master Jacob Frank taught that this lowly world is in thrall to evil beings who enslave us with death, sickness, and decay. These are the creatures of the law, of all those fine distinctions between the permitted and the prohibited—the gleeful spreaders of Adam's curse after he was driven forth from the Garden of Eden. And they too are led by a maiden. She appears righteous but is in fact wicked—she was once a servant of the true Holy Maiden but she treacherously usurped her mistress's rightful place.

Jacob Frank was imprisoned for thirteen years in the fortress at Czestochowa, until the Czar's troops freed him when they invaded Poland and seized the district. He then left Poland and established his court at Brno in Moravia, and later at Offenbach. He received many pilgrims who begged him for blessings and words of wisdom—wisdom often revealed through parables and anecdotes of his youth and accounts of his dreams. Long after these visits, his followers would tell each other tales of the master's wonders and teachings, of his greatness and wealth. There were even rumors that his daughter Ewa, who was said by some to be the incarnation of the Holy Maiden, had seduced and bewitched the Emperor of Austria, Joseph II.

My parents, like most of those Jews who had followed Jacob Frank and obeyed his command to be baptized, lived in Warsaw, where they owned a small shop. Outwardly, we pretended to be upright Christians, receiving communion and hearing Mass each Sunday morning. But inwardly, secretly, we maintained our faith in the teachings of Jacob Frank and his mission to free the Holy

Maiden and grant us the blessings of never-ending youth, health, and riches.

When I was a boy, my parents would often journey to the master's court. But they refused to take me with them, saying I was too young for such an arduous trip. And then our lord and master Jacob Frank died, still unable to reach the Holy Maiden and defeat the forces of death and decay. His faithful, his company of believers, including my parents, were inconsolable in their grief, for they knew that his death and failure were their fault. He had often bemoaned how his company of believers had failed him—how they had not been steadfast enough in their faith, too hesitant, too doubting, too weak for the great struggle in which he had tried to lead us. His blood was on our hands, for if we had only been stronger he would have reached the Holy Maiden, and she would have granted him her gifts of immortality, wealth, and eternal beauty.

By the time he died, I had grown to be a man. I said to my parents: *You* have failed our lord and master Jacob Frank. *You* did not redeem the Holy Maiden from her distant exile. Let me now go to Offenbach to learn the wisdom of our lady Ewa Frank, his daughter, and the other members of the holy company who yet remain there. Where you wavered, *my* faith will be steadfast and true.

Tortured by their guilt over the master's death, my parents agreed. They handed me a purse bursting with ducats to donate for the upkeep and glory of the lady Ewa's court and sent me on my way.

After a long journey, I arrived in Offenbach. But what I found there was not truth and freedom, but instead greed, lies, and corruption. The lady Ewa Frank and her brothers immediately took almost all my money—both my intended donation and then some. They then put me to work, toiling from dusk until dawn at menial tasks around their palace for no pay other than a few crusts of bread and a threadbare blanket crawling with lice.

I tolerated this rude treatment in the hopes of learning some great wisdom. But Ewa and her brothers never spoke any words of wisdom. Rather, they exploited the simple, passionate faith of their father's believers to raise donations that they wasted on expensive clothes, luxurious wines, and gilded carriages.

Filled with disgust, I left the lady Ewa and her false court. Nevertheless, I still longed for the freedom from bondage that Jacob Frank had taught and promised to us—I yearned for her, the Holy Maiden, to embrace my shivering, weeping soul and bless me with happiness and abundance. But how to find her? Where to find her?

And then I recalled the place where the revelation of the Holy Maiden had first come to Jacob Frank: the Jasna Gora monastery in Czestochowa, home to the famous painting of the Black Madonna. I resolved to travel myself to Czestochowa. Perhaps I would also be found worthy to have visions of my own.

When I arrived at Czestochowa, I told the monks that I was a pilgrim who wished to pray to the Madonna and seek her blessing. As I told you, my parents had followed Jacob Frank to the baptismal font and abandoned their Judaism. I had been baptized as a Catholic when I was an infant. Thus, to the monks, I was simply another pilgrim.

I had to wait several days before I was able to see the Black Madonna. There were long snaking lines of desperate pilgrims—all pleading with the Holy Virgin Mother to cure their afflictions or bless them with children—who jostled ahead of me. When my allotted time came at last, I walked slowly and humbly into the chapel and knelt down before the altar. On one side was a painting of St. Barbara and on the other side was a picture of St. Catherine.

And between them, rising above the altar, was the Black Madonna of Czestochowa, the miracle-working painting that drew so many pilgrims to this place—and that had stirred or guided the visions of Jacob Frank when he had been a prisoner at Czestochowa, his visions of the power and might of the Holy Maiden.

She did not resemble other paintings of the Virgin and Child. In other pictures I have seen, the Madonna is pale, fragile, and beset by an inconsolable sorrow. Her eyes saw only beloved, suffering children, and her heart yearned to heal and comfort them.

But the Black Madonna is different. Her skin is dark and her face is long, narrow, and grave. She neither exults nor weeps. There are gashes on her cheek, but they do not seem to bother her. Her slender lips are closed tightly and her gaze drifts off into the distance beyond. Her child, the infant Christ, is grabbing her dress and looking at her eagerly, lovingly—hungry for his mother's warmth—but she ignores him.

I knelt down before her, my hands clasped together in supplication, and looked up to meet her gaze. But I did not pray for health or children or even money. I prayed for her to reveal to me the secret of the Holy Maiden that she had revealed to our lord and master Jacob Frank when he, so many years before, had also knelt down before her.

As soon as I had finished my prayer, I heard a loud wind blow past my ears, as if a tremendous storm had burst forth inside the chapel. Yet when I looked around none of the objects in the chapel had stirred from its place, and the flames of the candles were burning gently and peacefully.

I felt a sudden chill in my bones, and an invisible hand grabbed the back of my head and tilted it so that I was looking directly into the eyes of the Black Madonna above the altar. And then I beheld the most extraordinary sight: The Black Madonna put her child down and stepped out of her painting, tall and resplendent. She floated down to me and placed her hands on my temples and squeezed them with a frightening, inhuman strength. I screamed in agony until I collapsed onto the ground.

While I was lying there in a stupor, I saw many visions of the Holy Maiden—as an ancient goddess, as a sorceress, as a prophetess, as a queen. She was terrifying in her beauty, and wherever she spread forth her hand she banished death and cured disease and brought forth abundance and wealth and beauty.

I also saw her wicked handmaiden, whose touch brought forth pestilence and death in the body and guilt and weeping in the soul. This handmaiden gathered around her an assembly of trembling little men with long white beards, scholars of the law, and together they waged war against the Holy Maiden and banished her beyond a boundary of some kind—a wall that seemed to be made of air, gentle and soft to the touch, but still somehow thick and impenetrable.

But then I saw something else—a castle in Poland, hundreds of years ago, where a noble lady resided and held court. At the touch of her hand, old men and women became young and beautiful once more and empty chests magically filled with gold coins. She was life and abundance incarnate—she was the Holy Maiden returned to this world.

The wicked handmaiden, though, in her fury at such life and joy, unleashed her knights, in their melancholy grey armor, to ride against the noble lady. I saw her cut down in her own courtyard, hacked to pieces by their swords.

The next thing I saw in my vision was a small chapel in the woods crowded with worshippers. On the altar sat an exquisitely carved box that was the color of moonlight and decorated with strange symbols etched in black. The lid of the box suddenly sprung open, and a human head floated up above the congregation—the head of the beautiful noblewoman who had been killed by the wicked knights in her courtyard. The head spoke and gave them her blessing.

However, the worshippers' joy was brief, because their chapel then burst into flames and, as the door had somehow been bolted shut to prevent their escape, I saw them all die a horrible death in the fire.

That was the end of my vision.

When I awoke again, I found myself lying in a narrow bed. The voices around me were groaning in pain and coughing miserably. Sitting up and looking around, I realized I had been taken to the infirmary where the monks tended to pilgrims who had fallen ill.

A young brother rushed to my side. He told me that I had suffered from a seizure while praying before the Black Madonna. He asked me if I had received a vision. He said that other pilgrims who had suffered similar seizures had beheld the Black Madonna walk out of her painting and show them wonders and marvels.

I knew better than to reveal the truth of what I had seen. Jacob Frank had been betrayed to the Church as a heretic shortly after his baptism, which is how he became a prisoner for so many years in the fortress at Czestochowa. He warned his company of believers never to divulge his teachings to the small-minded, cold-hearted men of the Church, as they were no better than the rabbis who persecuted him when he had been a Jew.

And so, I told the monk that I had seen the Holy Virgin Mother in Heaven surrounded by a group of saints, all holding hands and sweetly singing the praises of the Christ child. The monk clapped his hands, smiled broadly, and uttered heartfelt prayers of thanksgiving and joy.

Once I was sufficiently recovered, I left the monastery and returned to my inn. There, I sat alone in my attic room and tried to make sense of what I had seen in my vision. I was sure the Holy Maiden—who either was the Black Madonna or spoke through the Black Madonna—had revealed herself to me in her true splendor. I wondered about the lady in the castle whom the knights had killed— the lady whose severed head had magically blessed that congregation in the woods. Was she an incarnation of the Holy Maiden? What had happened to the box with her head in it—had it been destroyed in the fire, or had it survived?

Later in the evening, I came upon a couple of Gentile men drinking in the tavern in my inn. I asked them if they had ever heard of a chapel in the woods that had been used by a sect of heretics before being burned to the ground. While they both swore they had never heard of any such tale, one of them added that, if anything like that had ever happened, the monks would have recorded it in their chronicles, which were kept in the library at Jasna Gora.

I resolved to return to the monastery to study these chronicles. As it happened, the head librarian there had heard of my alleged vision of the Virgin Mother in Heaven from his brothers in the infirmary and was thus quite willing to let me peruse his library's books and manuscripts.

I now spent each day, from dawn until dusk, in the monks' library. I found where they kept their chronicles, which were all written out by hand. Fortunately, as my parents had educated me to be a Catholic gentleman, I have a firm command of Latin and I had no difficulty in reading the monks' manuscripts.

For several days, I searched in vain for an account of a Polish noblewoman or sect of heretics similar to what I had seen in my vision. I waded through tedious descriptions of Church councils and petty squabbles among the brothers about whether such and such a monk had properly attended to his chores, prayed with sufficient fervor, or failed to complete a penance. It was dispiriting to read how such men—men who should have roamed this Earth as the masters of the land, taking their pleasures wherever they chose— had been reduced to sniveling, backbiting wretches accusing one another of insufficient fealty to some prohibition or rule of discipline. Reading about the monks' pitiful, pinched lives, I understood how desperately mankind needs Jacob Frank's teachings to free ourselves from the shackles of these despotic rules about what is permitted and what is forbidden—rules that reduce mankind to a race of sickly, trembling maggots anxiously writhing about in the dirt and waiting for the release of death.

But then one morning, as I strode again to the shelves where the monks' chronicles were kept, I heard a faint humming. I followed the sound until I came upon a wooden box sitting on a table in a back corner. When I touched the lid, I saw the Black Madonna once more, standing before me in all her cold, imposing glory. But an instant later she vanished from my eyes.

I opened the box and found a manuscript inside. It was titled *A Brief and True Account of the Defeat of the Heretics of the Forest of W. as Recorded in the Year of Our Lord 1375*. As I started to read, I quickly realized that this manuscript recounted the very events that I had beheld in my vision. It began with a brief biography of a noblewoman named Countess K., who was famed in her day as the most beautiful lady in the Kingdom of Poland. Tragedy befell her: Her parents and two brothers died of an unspecified disease, all within the same week. This sudden misfortune prompted a spiritual crisis in the soul of the young countess. She refused to eat, prayed constantly in the family chapel, and mortified her flesh with a whip. She was convinced that she had committed some terrible sin that had been the cause of all of these deaths, and she was now desperate to repent.

The local Bishop, who was more practical than mystical, endeavored to persuade her to eat again and turn her thoughts to marriage and children, so she could continue her ancient and esteemed bloodline. But she spurned his counsel and demanded instead to spend her remaining days—which she was certain were quite few—in a convent purifying her soul and begging for God's forgiveness.

Countess K.'s excessive, fanatical penance finally caused her to fall ill with such a raging fever that she could not leave her bed. In her delirium, she repeatedly called out to a woman or a spirit whom she referred to as the Holy Maiden. The chronicler noted that while these statements were understood at the time to refer to the Holy Virgin Mary, subsequent events were to demonstrate that her interlocutor had been an entirely different, and far from holy, being.

And then one morning, her fever suddenly broke. The countess, miraculously restored to perfect health, now became, to everyone's shock, a voluptuary. She ate only the richest foods, flavored with the most exquisite spices, and washed them down with barrels of sweet Hungarian wine. She summoned the finest tailors to her castle and commissioned an array of silk dresses in dazzling colors—orange and yellow and pink and violet—that flattered and accentuated her beautiful form.

The Countess K. also opened the gates of her castle to her fellow nobles and hosted grand balls for their entertainment. The chronicler intimated that there were shameful acts of debauchery committed during these celebrations, but, as a pious and modest churchman, he did not elaborate.

The chronicler also recorded another unexpected change in the noble lady: The debauched Countess K. had acquired miraculous healing powers. She had cured a deathly ill servant with only the touch of her hand and her blessing. And not merely cured him, but the man now appeared to be several years younger and far more vigorous than he had ever been before. The castle servants spread the tale of this miracle far and wide and soon men and women of all ages, stations, and ranks sought her out as a healer.

And her ability to heal and revitalize extended beyond the human world. When she visited her fields, her presence would cause the crops to spring up suddenly in harvests more bountiful than ever before. Her touch would make horses stronger and livestock healthier and fatter.

Upon hearing of these miraculous acts, the Bishop and other authorities within the Church concluded that the Countess K. was a witch who had made a foul pact with the Devil. Otherwise, there was no explanation for how a vain, sinful woman like her could work such wonders—for surely God would only give such power to a humble and pious saint. According to the Church, her visions in her feverish delirium of a Holy Maiden must have been of a female demon who had successfully tempted her into surrendering her immortal soul. Thus, when she awoke from her fever, she abandoned her Christian morality for sin and sensuality, and could also wield supernatural powers newly granted to her by Lucifer.

The good men of the Church were duly alarmed. Who could say how many souls she could lead to sin and perdition, between the lure of her beauty and the wonders of her miraculous healing? They had to act. They called upon the aid of a neighboring landowner, an old widower of deep faith. His knights stormed into her castle as she was curing the sick in her courtyard and they quickly cut her down.

But now the tale took another strange turn. The chronicler recorded that the people of that district had been so thoroughly seduced by this emissary of the Devil that, instead of celebrating their freedom from her, they were stricken with an inconsolable grief. These mourners took to praying together in a small, long-abandoned chapel deep inside the forest.

Rumors soon spread that there was a sacred relic inside this chapel with miraculous powers to heal sickness, restore youth, and bestow wealth and worldly success. It was said that certain of the late Countess K.'s noble lovers, vile and unrepentant fornicators in the chronicler's view, had frequented the chapel in disguise to beseech the aid of this mysterious relic.

Even more concerning to the pious chronicler, these former lovers and other followers of the dead countess were soon conspicuous for their remarkable good fortune—illnesses healed, wrinkled faces and flabby figures returned to the vigor and beauty of youth. Wealth, abundant wealth, showered down upon them: The estates of her former lovers enjoyed bountiful harvests and fat livestock, and several of her followers suddenly came into large and unexpected inheritances.

To the sober leaders of the Church, this was all proof that the malevolent influence of Lucifer remained all too strong in this district. To them, the only reasonable explanation for such otherwise inexplicable good fortune was that these persons—all of them—were bartering their souls to the Devil. The Bishop decided to send a spy to the chapel in the forest, a servant whom he had only recently brought into his service from a faraway town and who accordingly was not known to the people in the district. This spy reported back that the congregation in the chapel worshipped a box placed upon an altar. This box was the color of moonlight and had markings in black that he could not decipher. The worshippers would approach the box, one by one, kiss it, and beseech it for some boon—wealth, beauty, health, and so on and so forth.

When they were all finished, they returned to their seats in the pews. And then the lid of the box opened of its own accord. A severed head—a beautiful, aristocratic lady's head, young and lovely with thick, lustrous golden hair—floated up into the air from the box and spoke aloud various blessings. After she was finished, the head returned to her box.

The Bishop decided to act once more to smite the evil in his midst. He mustered a troop of pious knights, whose faith in Christ was incorruptible, and they departed in the daytime to lie in wait in the woods near the chapel, concealing themselves within the dense foliage. That evening, after the congregation had filed into the chapel for what the chronicler called their abominable demonic rites, the knights left their hiding places, bolted and locked the door to the chapel from the outside, and then set fire to the building. Her followers all died in the blaze.

The next morning, a young knight found the enchanted box on top of the pile of charred ruins. But when he tried to touch it, the box burrowed itself deep into the ground. The monk concluded his account by giving thanks to God that the knights' brave assault upon the minions of Hell had put an end to the worship of Lucifer in the district.

When I finished reading this chronicle, I was trembling with excitement. The Black Madonna and the Countess K. were both obviously aspects of, or reflections of, the Holy Maiden whom our lord and master Jacob Frank had venerated. I had been shown a way to find the Holy Maiden and harness her power. I merely had to discover where the magical box was buried.

I reread the monk's chronicle several times, looking for any clue as to the location where these events had taken place. Eventually, through much subtle and intense probing, I figured out the district and made plans to travel there. But first, I returned home to Warsaw to prepare for the journey. While in Warsaw, I disclosed my intended itinerary to an acquaintance who works in the royal treasury. He then told me that the lord of that district was staying in Warsaw.

You have already heard from the *Pan* how I approached him in Warsaw and won his confidence. And now we shall find the Holy Maiden's enchanted box and summon her back to this world. We will revel in her blessings and her gifts and be freed from our chains.

V. The Blessings of Matrimony

AFTER HEARING ALL this crazy nonsense from Pawel's lips, I was terrified that such a man—a mad heretic descended from umpteen generations of other mad heretics—had now become the *Pan*'s closest counselor. After the persecutions—just as they were—that Pawel and his forefathers had suffered at the hands of the righteous rabbis of Poland, he would be no friend to our town's Jews.

I was eager to get away from him so I could go home and warn the community elders and our rabbi. But before I could rid myself of his company, I had to find a mound of dirt for him large enough that he could believe it to be the remains of the church burned down in the forest so long ago, as the monk had written it. Thinking quickly as the wagon rounded a sharp bend in the road, I recalled there was a clearing with a high mound near where we were in the forest. So, I told the driver to stop the wagon and wait for us.

Pawel, I said, I think the place you are looking for is close. Follow me.

Pawel leapt out of his seat, practically panting, and followed me through the narrow and overgrown footpaths. After a couple of minutes, we reached a wide clearing. In the exact center of the clearing, just as I remembered it, stood a high, circular dirt mound—easily three times the height of a grown man.

Pawel screeched for joy and raced up the mound. When he reached the top, he laid down on the ground and pushed his ear deep into a patch of dirt, as if he were straining to listen to some sound coming from deep inside the mound. He looked to me like a lunatic—after all, what did he expect the dirt to say to him?

Eventually, he stood up again and ran back down the side of the mound to the level ground where I was standing. Grinning like an old drunken peasant, he said to me: My dear friend Aryeh Lieb, this is the place. There can be no doubt of it. The chapel was said to be situated in the exact center of a wide clearing, just like that mound. And the wicked men who persecuted her, the Holy Maiden, they buried her box and her chapel beneath a great pile of dirt. But behold—she is life itself—she is youth and beauty, and she gives her gifts generously. That is why all the bushes bloom so gloriously upon her mound, a song in color to exalt her name and glory.

I told him that I was glad to have found just the place he was looking for, and I wished him luck in digging up his magic box. However, I added, it was long past time for me to return home—my wife was no doubt worried that something terrible might have happened to me.

Pawel agreed I could go back home so long as the wagon driver would return later with more men and plenty of shovels to dig up the mound. He added that he intended to stay right where he was in the clearing and pray to his Holy Maiden.

So, I bid him farewell and returned to the wagon, which had been waiting on the side of the forest road. I told the driver first to take me home and then to return to this spot by the clearing with workers and tools. He asked me why anyone would want to dig up a mound of dirt, but I said this was the *Pan*'s will and that was that.

The wagon arrived at my home in the early afternoon. I felt such joy as you could not imagine when I once again kissed my own *mezuzah* on my own doorpost. My Miriam must have heard my footsteps, because I heard her drop a pan on the ground, and then she rushed over to me, with our little children hanging onto her legs. Her eyes looked exhausted from worry, and there were dried tears on her cheeks.

She said to me: *Baruch Ha-Shem,* you are home! And in one piece! I was so scared—I read your note this morning—you said the *Pan* had dragged you out of bed in the middle of the night, to take you to his house—I could not imagine—I have heard stories of drunken noblemen setting their black dogs on Jewish leaseholders—I could not imagine—but you are here—the Holy One, Blessed be He, has heard my prayers and returned you safely to us. But you look so tired. Did you sleep? What did they do to you? No—don't say anything, you must eat something first. Come with me.

And then she grabbed me by the hand, dragged me into the kitchen, and shoved me down into a wooden chair next to our big table. She poured me a glass of brandy and served a steaming bowl of borscht with her wonderfully thick sour cream. And there was something else, too—yes, black bread and onions.

When I was finished—and I wasted no time devouring that meal—she spoke up again: So, what happened? Tell me. I am being eaten alive by my worries.

I yawned loudly—for the brandy and sour cream had made me drowsy—and then I told her all that I had heard and seen. When I was finished, she said it was a miracle that I had escaped unharmed from that crazy Pawel—may *HaShem* curse all the mad, wicked degenerates who follow liars and frauds like Jacob Frank.

Later that night, when I was lying down in bed, I distinctly recall Miriam spreading the blanket over me and thinking: No woman could be as pleasing to me as my Miriam with her soft, plump flesh, so warm when I nuzzled my cheek against her. And unlike the grand ladies of Warsaw who tormented the old *Pan,* she did not care if I grew old and perhaps was no longer as handsome as I was on the day we stood under the *chuppah*.

That thought about standing under the *chuppah* dredged up my memories of our wedding night. Between the loud music and the well-wishers and the presentation of gifts and all the drunken old Jews who had to sprinkle their very own special crumb of wisdom over our heads, the two of us, the bride and groom, were barely able to speak to each other during the day of our wedding. But eventually later on, when everyone else had gone away, we found ourselves alone in our new marriage bed. Although I knew what I had to do, I was terrified. Trembling, I reached out for Miriam's hand. She grabbed my hand tightly and pulled me close to her. I snuggled against her warm flesh and looked up at her kind brown eyes. She stroked my cheek and kissed my lips, a kiss that sent shivers of joy through all my limbs. From that moment, I have loved her more than my words could ever say—she is my *bashert*, my destined bride and my one true beloved. Whenever I have despaired, her touch and her smile would restore me to a happiness so sweet that it must have been a foretaste of the delights of Paradise in the World to Come.

The next morning, as soon as I entered the synagogue for my morning prayers, I was immediately surrounded by the rabbi and the other leading householders in the town. They had all apparently heard about how the *Pan* had summoned me to his manor house in the dead of night and they wanted to know what had happened. After I had recounted to them what I had heard and seen from Pawel and the *Pan*, the other householders raised their hands up towards the roof, wailing in despair, and asked one another how could their lord and protector have fallen under the sway of a follower of Jacob Frank and Sabbatai Zevi, the false Messiahs, the wicked charlatans? And what was going to happen when this Pawel failed to find—because of course it could not exist—this ridiculous *meshuggeneh* magic box?

Still, over the next few days, everybody calmed down. No one else was rustled out of his bed in the middle of the night. Whatever your father, the old *Pan*, was doing, he was doing it far away from his Jews and our *shtetl*.

VI. When the Hound Sniffs Blood

NOW THAT I was left alone again, I turned my thoughts away from Pawel and Holy Maidens and magic boxes and back towards harvesting timber and shipping and selling the wood. Time passed—at least weeks, maybe months. I can't recall exactly anymore. As there were no more orders from the *Pan*—or even a letter from him—I began to hope that he had recovered his reason and thrown Pawel out of his house. Maybe even, should I be so lucky, His Lordship had decided to depart for some great city far away where he could once more chase after beautiful *shikse* noblewomen.

But then one morning, when I was entering the synagogue courtyard, I came upon a crowd of Jews tugging wildly at their beards and *peyes*. In between their howling and moaning, they were asking each other the same question over and over again: *But who could he possibly be?*

I pushed my way to the front of the crowd, and there I beheld a horrible sight: A dead body was lying on the ground, naked and covered with animal bites, as if the corpse had been spat out from the lion's den in Babylon. He did not look Jewish—no beard, no *peyes*. However, the note in Polish nailed to his left temple read: This is one of yours, put him in the Jewish cemetery.

Something about him seemed familiar, so I decided to have a closer look. I bent down until my nose was practically touching the face of the dead man.

And then I realized who it was: The dead man was Pawel.

I stumbled backwards into the crowd, fell to the ground, and vomited. When I stood back up, I told the other Jews to quiet down, as I knew who this was. The dead man, I said to them, was the follower of Sabbatai Zevi and Jacob Frank who had been the *Pan*'s guest and companion. This was the madman who had ranted about Holy Maidens and magic boxes.

The other householders then asked me—as I, alone among them, had known this Pawel—to go visit the *Pan*'s manor house and humbly request His Lordship's guidance on how we should dispose of the body and whether there would be an investigation into the circumstances of his death. We wanted to be careful not to offend our lord, as we assumed he would be distressed and angry to learn of his friend's death.

While I was not happy to be entangled again in the affairs of Pawel and the old *Pan*—whatever they might be—it was true that I was in the best position to manage this delicate circumstance. And so, after quickly reciting my morning prayers, I went with a heavy heart to the stables by the inn and hired a coachman to take me to the manor house.

When I arrived, the *Pan* was away. The servants said he had ridden out the night before with a large hunting party, and they were all going to spend the next few nights in an old lodge in the woods. But the steward had remained behind and could receive me. The servants then led me to the back room where the steward transacted business on behalf of the estate, a room that I had visited many times before.

After we had both sat down, the steward asked what urgent matter had brought me there unannounced.

I recounted for him how several Jews and I had come upon Pawel's corpse in the synagogue courtyard. I said the elders of the Jewish community respectfully sought the guidance of the *Pan* as to how to handle the remains of His Lordship's close companion and whether there would be an inquiry into the circumstances of Pawel's death. We, of course, would gladly provide our complete cooperation in any investigation that His Lordship might choose to undertake.

The steward did not respond at first. He turned his eyes to the ceiling and seemed to be silently debating some intricate, subtle point inside his head. After a while, he turned back to me and this is what he said: Aryeh Lieb, my friend, there will be no inquiry into this death. Consider yourself fortunate that the *Pan* has departed for the hunt and you are asking me these questions, and not him. I cannot recall—when did you and Pawel part ways? Was that before or after they found the box?

I said that, as far as I knew, neither Pawel nor anyone else had ever found any magic box. I had shown him the clearing with the tall mound in the middle and then returned home. And afterwards, thankfully, no one had troubled me any further with crazy nonsense about boxes and Holy Maidens.

But the steward looked at me gravely, shook his head, and then he continued: After you departed, Pawel organized a band of peasants to dig up that mound. They shoveled and hauled dirt for three, four, maybe even five days. It was backbreaking work—that soil was packed in densely, almost as hard as a rock. In the end, they found the buried remains of an ancient, decrepit altar. And on top of the altar, they found a box. It was the color of a brightly glowing moon and around the sides there were etchings in black—some strange sort of writing that no one could decipher.

Pawel was overjoyed and immediately proclaimed this to be the very box from his vision at Czestochowa. He was sure the Holy Maiden's magically preserved, severed head was inside this box and that by means of this ghastly relic he could commune with her and conjure her power and blessings.

But before they could harness its power, they had to figure out how to open it. This proved to be no easy task. As the box had clearly visible grooves, it seemed that the lid should flip right open. Yet no man on the estate could pry it open. They tried all sorts of means to break it open—they swung an axe, they shot at it with pistols, and they even threw it into a raging fire.

But the box remained stubbornly closed, without even a dent or a scratch.

Pawel then attempted a new approach. He went alone into the *Pan*'s private chapel and locked himself inside for three days and three nights. Refusing all offers of food and drink, he prayed so loudly that we could hear him clearly through the thick doors. But his prayers were neither Jewish nor Christian. Rather, he prayed to his Holy Maiden, whom he seemed to conflate, at least sometimes, with the Holy Virgin Mother.

When he finally left the chapel, Pawel staggered back to the *Pan* and announced that he had learned the secret of the box. The Holy Maiden had appeared to him in a new vision in which she explained the meaning of the symbols etched in black around the box. As a result, he now knew how to open it, although first he needed to eat and drink to restore his strength.

After Pawel had eaten an ample meal and indulged in a long nap, the *Pan* ordered several members of his household, myself included, to gather around him and Pawel in the parlor room. Pawel placed the box down upon a table directly beneath the chandelier and then walked around it in a circle reciting strange words that made no sense to me.

After a while, a black smoke began to seep forth from underneath the box's lid. But it was not hot and it did not smell like fire. Instead, it had a sweet, gentle scent that could lull one to sleep.

I was reminded of the lotus-eaters from Homer's *Odyssey*, but I suppose that means nothing to you as a Jew.

After the smoke had been leaking out for a few minutes, the lid of the box suddenly opened of its own accord. A woman's severed head emerged from inside the box and rose into the air above us. This head was strikingly beautiful—thick golden hair, rosy cheeks, full and sensuous lips. And when her eyes opened, they were wide and dark blue and burning with passion.

The head looked around the room until she spied Pawel. She then glided over to him and feverishly kissed his lips. Once she was finished, she went back inside her box, and the lid promptly closed again.

Pawel fell down unconscious upon the floor. The *Pan* ordered that Pawel be carried to his bed to rest, but that no doctor should be summoned. He also made sure the box was secured in a locked cabinet to which he had the only key.

Around noon the next day, Pawel awoke again. He was not only restored to perfect health, but he appeared far more handsome than before—his features had been altered somehow, imperceptibly, subtly, but the effect overall was undeniable. And his shoulders had broadened and his muscles were larger.

Full of newfound vigor, he ran from his bed, still half naked, out of the manor house towards the stables. In the yard there, we had a new stallion, a wild young thing. He was not yet broken in, and we had to keep him tied to a post with a thick rope. Pawel jumped on the back of this vicious beast, without a saddle, broke the knot around his neck, and rode the wild horse across the meadow that stretches out between the house and the forest. The horse repeatedly tried to throw him to the ground. I was sure the mad fool was going to get his neck broken. But Pawel held on and rode the horse and broke him in. In the end, the defeated stallion trotted meekly back to the stables and submitted without protest to being yoked again to his post.

With sweat rolling down his naked torso, and a broad grin on his face, Pawel now strode over to the group of us who had been watching him from the veranda. The women in the household stared after him with a panting, animal lust. But Pawel laughed at them and loudly demanded a loaf of bread and a mug filled with beer.

I turned my eyes to the *Pan*. He was looking at Pawel, too, but he did not look pleased with Pawel's triumph—no, he appeared to me to be lost in his own brooding thoughts, angry thoughts. Still, at the time, he said nothing. Later that afternoon, he asked Pawel to teach him the secret of summoning the lady's head from the box. Pawel resisted at first—perhaps he also had a foreboding of something evil in His Lordship's eyes—but then the *Pan* told Pawel that he had arranged for the box to be hidden away and secured under lock and key. If Pawel ever wished to taste again the sweet favors of his Holy Maiden, he needed to reveal what the *Pan* wished to know.

Thus, Pawel, with a heavy sigh, followed the *Pan* into the far back wing of the house, where they remained alone together for a long time. There were occasional strange shouts, or maybe they were chants, but otherwise there was no indication of whatever it was they were doing there.

After they emerged again, the *Pan* ordered us all to assemble once more in the parlor room. He had Pawel bound to a chair with thick ropes—thicker than the ropes that had been used with the wild horse—and his mouth was stuffed with a gag so that he could neither speak any incantation nor receive another kiss from that beautiful head. Once these preparations were complete, the *Pan* retrieved the magic box and placed it back again on the same table beneath the chandelier.

Now it was His Lordship who circled the box and recited strange words in a bizarre tongue. The box again breathed out its sweet smoke and then opened by itself. This time the lovely head kissed the *Pan* until she had tasted her full and returned to her box.

After the lid closed above her, the *Pan* collapsed, although the servants caught him before he hit the floor.

And just as it had happened with Pawel, when he awoke again after an unnaturally long slumber, the *Pan* was a stronger and more vigorous man than he had ever been before. He looked ten, maybe even fifteen years younger—and never had he appeared so handsome. His chest and arms bulged with newfound power and he was able to swing the heaviest axes like they were tiny sticks. And like Pawel, he too enjoyed the adoring, hungry glances and heavy breathing of the women in the household.

For the next several weeks, the two men were the greatest of friends. They rode together, they hunted together, they amused each other shooting off pistols, and they took turns using the box. As they grew stronger, the fainting spells lessened and eventually ceased altogether.

They also pursued some sort of secret, occulted ritual. I cannot describe what it was—suffice to say, I was never invited to partake of this rite. They would dress themselves in animal hides—wolf skins, usually—and lock themselves inside the manor house's private chapel with the magic box for hours on end. Through the doors I could hear that they were chanting and moaning, whether in pleasure or pain I could not tell. After a while, they began to take a young maid who worked on the household staff, a pretty thing with blonde hair and rosy cheeks, with them into the chapel. She, too, would moan, and sometimes scream. When they left the chapel, her hair would be tousled and her clothes slightly ripped, but she would not speak of what had happened. Her eyes seemed to stare off at a distant horizon only visible to her, and she would shiver and mumble nonsense sounds and caress her hands all over her body as if she were trying to soothe herself somehow. Yet she never resisted His Lordship's command to return with him and Pawel to that chapel and continue whatever foul crimes were being done against her honor and modesty.

But then the *Pan* turned against Pawel.

A young widow with a small estate near this district, a lady of ancient and noble blood but little money, had learned of the *Pan*'s return to his country estate after his extended absence in Warsaw and abroad. Delighted at last to have an aristocratic neighbor to call upon, she arranged to pay us a visit for a few days.

Both Pawel and the *Pan* were instantly smitten with her. She, in turn, was overjoyed to chance upon two such handsome men in her rustic wasteland, as she put it. She played the coquette now with the one and then with the other. I had the impression that she enjoyed this sport so much that she did not want to have to choose either man as her lover.

But then on the last night of her visit, she did yield her favors— to Pawel. No doubt aware that this triumph would arouse the *Pan*'s jealousy, Pawel had arranged for a secret rendezvous in the wine cellars at midnight, where he thought he could act unobserved. Yet despite Pawel's careful precautions, His Lordship still learned of their assignation. Perhaps one of the older servants, those grim and silent men who had so loyally served his father and even his grandfather, sniffed out and betrayed Pawel's secret.

The lovely coquette returned to her own estate the morning after she had taken her pleasure with Pawel. The next day after that, when Pawel sat down at the long table for the midday meal, he drank one cup of the drugged wine and then immediately collapsed onto the floor.

When Pawel awoke again, he was lying naked on the floor, bound fast with iron chains, in the same cellar where he had enjoyed such exquisite sensual delights with the young widow. The *Pan* was there, too, standing over him and waiting for him to stir back to consciousness. Once he was sure that Pawel was fully alert, he whistled to his three black hunting dogs. They pounced upon Pawel and tore his flesh to pieces while His Lordship watched.

And then I presume some servant, acting on the *Pan*'s orders, dropped the corpse in the synagogue courtyard. You Jews had better dispose of it, and quickly. I cannot imagine that His Lordship wishes for any questions to be asked.

Hearing this wild tale from the steward, I trembled with fright. I remember thinking: This woman in the box must be some sort of demon—some daughter of Lilith—set loose by that crazy fool Pawel. And now the *Pan* had been seduced by the demon and was in her power. What was the steward's role in all of this? Why hadn't he alerted his priests and monks to this danger? Surely, they must have their ways of expelling demons, just as a holy *tzaddik* or *baal shem* wages war against demons on behalf of Jews. Or was the steward simply trying to stay alive and avoid the murderous wrath of his master? Maybe he wished to warn us Jews—and others—of what had happened, so that we would take measures to fight the demon?

Still, I decided I should not let my tongue be too loose with the steward. And so, I said back to him: Sir, I will follow your counsel and make sure that Pawel's body is buried quickly and discreetly.

The steward nodded his head and bid me farewell.

VII. A New Adam Asserts His Dominion Over Every Living Thing

AFTER I RETURNED to my *shtetl* and informed the other Jewish householders of all that I had learned, a terrible panic set in—for who could say what crimes the demon-infatuated *Pan* might be tempted to undertake. Vigorous steps were taken to safeguard our community: Pawel's body was immediately buried in an unmarked grave just beyond the cemetery fence; all women who were not yet aged or infirm—even those who were married—were ordered by the rabbi to stay inside their homes as much as possible, cover their heads with ugly, preferably soiled, kerchiefs, wear modest and ill-fitting clothes, and otherwise to do everything in their power to make themselves appear as undesirable as possible to the lustful, mad nobleman; and the men set up a system of watches at night, in case the *Pan* and his dogs should descend upon the town.

A messenger was also dispatched to a *shtetl* two towns over, where a young but already famous *tzaddik* resided, a holy saint who had studied at the feet of the great master and teacher, the light of the Exile and pillar of his generation, Rebbe Levi Yitzhak. After hearing of how the lord who ruled our town had been seduced by a she-demon, the *tzaddik* came at once to our *shtetl* to direct our spiritual resistance. He wrote out amulets with powerful combinations of holy names to ward off demons; he made a thorough inspection of the scrolls inside each *mezuzah* on every Jewish doorpost, to make sure there were no blemishes that could permit a demon to enter the home; and he led all-night prayer *minyanim* to implore the aid of the Holy One, Blessed be He, for His beleaguered people Israel in the face of such danger.

And, *baruch HaShem*, our prayers were heard and our precautions kept the demon away from us. But the Christian peasants were not so fortunate. For, as I heard from my Gentile foreman and laborers, there were horrible crimes happening all over the countryside. When the moon was high in the sky and the peasants in their huts were drifting off to sleep, there would suddenly be a mad howling and barking. But these howls and barks did not sound like the wild animals. They were almost human, but still somehow inhuman—like a pack of demons were out riding in the woods.

The next morning, the peasants would find their livestock gone or dead. Or their vegetable patches trampled or even burned. In despair at the loss of the food they would need for the coming winter, the peasants stormed the manor house. With tears in their eyes, they pleaded for help.

But, as my foreman told the tale to me, the *Pan* was nowhere to be seen and the steward would not look them in the eye. He seemed embarrassed, even ashamed, as if it was he who had conjured the devils and needed to atone for his sins. He mumbled vague intentions about seeing what could be done and then dismissed the peasants from his sight.

And then the evil spirits, or whatever they were, committed a far more shameful crime. A pretty young maiden had gone into the forest to gather sour cherries for her mother's preserves. But she did not return to her parents until the following morning. And when she did come home, her dress was torn, her hair was a mess, and her face was covered with streaks of dried tears and dried blood. She walked slowly, shaking with terror. For a long time, she would not speak.

Her father sent for the priest, and the priest finally persuaded her to talk. And this is the tale she told: As the sun was setting, a rider on a horse came up beside her, threw a hood over her head, and grabbed her. The rider bound her wrists and carried her away. She was forced to drink a sickly-sweet but powerful liquor under the thick hood, and then she quickly fell asleep.

When she awoke, the hood was gone from her head, but she now found herself tied up and lying on the floor of a wide room with bare dark wooden walls. There was a dim light from a candle nearby. A group of men—or maybe they were demons or spirits—surrounded her. They had the bodies of men, but their heads looked like wolves.

Then came the most astonishing part of her tale. A woman's head that had been severed from its body—although it was still exceptionally beautiful, like a princess—was floating in the air inside the room. The head flew over to the young peasant girl, and then sniffed her, licked her cheek, and whispered something into her ear, but the words were garbled or maybe in some strange language she did not understand.

When the head was finished, it floated up to the top of the high wooden beams on the ceiling and let out a shrieking, piercing cry. As if they were dogs obeying their master's call, the wolf men immediately pounced upon the young maiden and assaulted her, committing abominable, horrible sins. Mercifully, she lost consciousness. She awoke the next morning back on the forest path, right at the spot where she had been abducted.

About a week after my foreman had told me this tale, I was awoken in the middle of the night by a loud screaming and howling. Wiping the sleep from my heavy eyes, I walked over to the window in my bedroom. My eyes smarted from a bright orange light outside—torches much brighter than the moon in the sky. I saw four men on horseback, wearing wolf hides, who were circling my house.

And then I heard someone trying to push open my front door. I rushed downstairs, still in my night clothes, and there I saw that one of the riders had overpowered the lock and forced his way inside. My Miriam followed me downstairs, and she screamed when she saw the rider with the wolfskin.

The rider spoke Polish; he told to be quiet. Then he said to me that the *Pan* wished to speak at once with his Jewish leaseholder, Aryeh Lieb. I was ordered to go upstairs and dress quickly.

When we were back upstairs in our bedroom, Miriam begged me not to go, as she feared I would not return to her alive—she would be a widow, and our children would be orphans. How could I go back to that demon-infested manor house? Was my heart made of stone?

But I said to her: I must do what I have to do. And I will come home again—for the Holy One, Blessed be He, is more powerful than any demon or nobleman. We must trust in His Mercy and His Protection.

And with that, I went down the staircase again and told the rider that I was ready to depart. By the time we were leaving, a huge crowd of Jews had gathered around my house, silent and trembling.

The riders told them to disperse.

All of the mute Jewish eyes turned to me.

I told them to go home and back to their beds. I said that I had visited the *Pan* many times before and I would be fine.

Then, in the blink of an eye, we were off, with me riding on the saddle behind one of the men in the wolfskins. With my heart pounding in terror, we raced through the roads in the darkness, until the horse suddenly halted in front of the manor house. The rider jumped off the horse onto the ground and grabbed me by the shoulder, pulling me crashing down into the dirt. After I got up and dusted myself off, the riders led me through the front door and into the parlor room.

There, I saw the *Pan* lounging on a couch, with a long dagger in his hands. Despite the late hour, he was wide awake. When we entered, the *Pan* stood up and dismissed the riders, saying he wished to speak to me alone. His Lordship directed me to sit down in a chair in the middle of the room, while he now walked over to the fireplace. For a while, he glared at me in silence. I wondered if he was weighing whether to stab me with his dagger. But then, the *Pan* spoke:

Aryeh Lieb, my fine leaseholder, thank you for answering my summons so promptly and deigning to call upon me at such a late hour. I have urgent business to discuss with you, business in which I shall require your most steadfast and loyal assistance.

I have learned much new wisdom since you last called upon me. I now understand the foolishness and the pettiness with which I have wasted away so many of my days—days spent in bondage to demonic powers that would have me grovel at their feet like a crippled serf, begging for alms. For too long I had felt the weight of the iron chains on my feet and struggled to break free. I refused to bow to that loathsome shrew whom my father forced me to wed. And then I wandered abroad, because I thought that Poland was my prison, and that if only I could reach a new shore—in Vienna, in Italy—I would be a free man. But the chains followed me wherever I went. They spoiled all my pleasures, torturing me with guilt and regret. I concealed these shameful, womanish feelings behind the mask of a cynical braggart and libertine, a would-be scheming seducer with a heart of ice. But those were all lies. I struggled for my freedom, but the chains—those laws of Christian morality, of decent society, natural laws, ecclesiastical laws, they all pulled at me until I fell to the ground.

But my friend Pawel had been brought up in the light of truth—the teachings of his parents' master, that heretic Jew Jacob

Frank. And when I too learned the wisdom of Jacob Frank, I was able at last to break free.

And I am also in your debt, Aryeh Lieb. You brought us to the mound in the forest. I could never have found it on my own—all those years in foreign climes had left me ignorant of my own ancestral lands. But you, my fine leaseholder, my master of timber and logs, know every inch of these woods. We dug up that mound and there we found the box—*her* box.

I have summoned her forth from the box many times. No mortal woman who lives and breathes has a head so beautiful and lustrous. Nor has any artist, no matter how accomplished or inspired, ever captured such an image in marble or oils. She is the divine Holy Maiden, the hidden goddess—the female spirit of God in your demented *kabbalah*, maybe even the Venus who lured Tannhauser into her cavern of delights.

When I first looked into the eyes of that eternally lovely face— a face that time cannot ravage—I fell instantly and madly in love with her and begged for her love in return. But she merely smiled and said back to me: I will give you something sweeter than my love—I will give you the wisdom that will free you from your chains.

But puffed up with my arrogant pride, I said I had no chains to break and needed no new wisdom—I needed only the love of the most perfect woman, a woman so much purer, so much rarer, in her beauty than the painted coquettes who prance and tease their way through the fashionable salons of Europe.

She laughed at me and retreated back inside her box. I collapsed in a swoon, and I slept the blackest sleep. But that sleep was a rebirth. When I opened my eyes, I felt a strength in my limbs that I had never felt before. I went straightaway to my stables, had my biggest and strongest stallion saddled, and then I rode him harder and faster than I had ever ridden a horse before—across streams, between thick trees, and trampling over bushes.

And as I rode, I felt another new sensation: That I was the master of all I surveyed. Obviously, I had long known myself to be the rightful, legal owner of this estate. But now the land belonged to me as my hands and my feet belong to me—as appendages that exist only to serve me and do my will.

It was *she* who had blessed me with this newfound power. And so, when I next summoned her forth from her box, I expressed my deep and profound gratitude for these wondrous gifts and, once again, I begged for her love.

Her red lips floated through the air until they were right next to my ear, and then they whispered to me: Man was created in the divine image to rule the world as its lord and master. That is how Adam lived in the Garden of Eden. He was given dominion over the whole Earth—over the fish in the sea, the birds in the sky, the animals that lumber across the land, and the creatures that creep through the dirt and the mud. When Adam was born from the dust, he was given no laws or prohibitions. He did as he willed, and he knew nothing of remorse or guilt. But then Eve and the serpent tempted him to eat the fruit that brought exile from Eden and death, sickness, and bitter toil to the world. And with death came prohibitions and commandments and shame. But these are the lies and illusions that shackle you and demean you. Have you ever felt guilty for taking your pleasures, for exercising your will? Those feelings are your chains rattling. Break them.

And then she fell silent again and the beautiful head drifted back inside her enchanted box.

I spent the next several days pondering her words. I had, all my life, endeavored to assert my will and take my pleasures. But I was always held back somehow—sometimes by the scornful glares and sharp rebukes of others, and sometimes by my own timidity and shame. I was compelled to admit to myself that I was not the fearless, cold libertine whom I pretended to be in society, but rather a guilt-ridden, hesitant coward.

I summoned her forth from her box once more. This time when I spoke to her, I burst into tears and made full confession of my wretchedness. I groveled upon the ground and implored her to redeem me from my lowly state.

But she is not a goddess of sorrow or compassion. Her face darkened with rage and she told me that I would not be freed from bondage until I could do more than conquer my guilt and my shame—I must blot them out entirely, from even the tiniest corners of my soul.

She said to me: You are the new Adam. You have dominion over everything you see and hear and touch. *Take* as you please.

And then she left me once more.

Turning her wise teachings over in my mind, I decided to exercise my dominion. I took my pleasures with the prettiest servant girls in my manor house and my villages. Sometimes they yielded themselves willingly; sometimes they resisted; but I no longer cared—I no longer desired to seduce and entice them to surrender their virtue. I willed it, and that was all.

I also seized cattle and pigs from my peasants to feast upon at my table. When they pleaded with me for redress and compensation, I tossed their petitions into the fire.

Pawel and I took to summoning her forth from her box in my private chapel. She would spit upon the crucifixes and statues of Mother Mary. She taught us certain rituals to draw down more of her strength, her power, into our flesh. But these rituals sometimes required us to make use of others, to bring—but never mind, you are not worthy of hearing such secrets.

The next time I summoned her by myself, without Pawel, she looked at me with eyes full of admiration and esteem. Her lips pressed hard against mine and she praised me for smashing my chains. However, she warned me that my final and most difficult test was approaching. If I should surmount this challenge, then I would finally be a man as Adam was meant to be, free of death and sickness and rules and restraints. I would be forevermore young, beautiful, and strong.

I asked her what this test was or at least by what signs I could recognize it when it came. But she did not answer me. Instead, she kissed me again, with a passion greater than any mortal woman could ever muster, and then disappeared back into her box.

Throughout this time, my closest companion had been my friend Pawel. Nevertheless, the last test was fated to be a struggle with him. The Lady Aleksandra K., a young widow of distinguished birth whose estate abuts my own, did me the kindness of paying a visit for several days. From the moment she crossed my threshold, both Pawel and I desired her. She, ever the coquette, flirted shamelessly with us both, now favoring one, and then the other. But she refused to yield her favors. I was tempted simply to take what I desired, but the Lady Aleksandra is a noblewoman—there could be consequences—I feared my dominion, alas, is perhaps not quite that absolute.

I sensed that she inclined more towards Pawel than me. I tasked a trustworthy old servant with watching them. From this old servant, I learned that during her final night at my house she gave herself to Pawel. He had wisely tried to conceal this assignation from me—the lovers met in secret, under cover of night. But the eyes of my watchful servants saw everything.

I was seething with jealousy and rage. I was stronger than ever, handsomer than ever, and yet I could not even seduce a lonely widow in the country? She was not even that pretty. If she were to set foot in a salon in Warsaw or Vienna or St. Petersburg, no one would look twice at her. But out here, surrounded by peasant girls stinking of garlic and smeared with grease and manure, she passed for a veritable Helen of Troy.

Reeling from my defeat, I considered once more whether I was perhaps just another pitiful ageing libertine, his charms fading fast beneath his swelling belly and spreading wrinkles. Soon enough the favors of even a middling lady would only be mine in exchange for a steep payment. I would decline into a vain old fool, still trying to rouge my cheeks and squeeze my corpulent, swollen flesh into tightly fashionable clothes.

Making matters worse, Pawel was now filled with such overbearing, smug pride at his petty conquest. While he said nothing, I saw him leering and smirking at the servant girls like a jaded libertine who fancies himself to be an expert seducer. He began to study his appearance in the mirror perhaps a bit too long and lovingly. He even made inquiries about tailors in the area—he no doubt thought that his wardrobe should be improved, the better to beguile his next conquest.

In my despair and bitterness, I went to the room where I kept the magic box. After making sure I was completely alone, I locked the door so no one could disturb me, and then I summoned her forth. I poured out my sufferings to her and cursed myself as a weak, deluded, pitiable wretch.

As I spoke, her eyes flared with rage, and, once I had finished my lament, she addressed me in a voice brimming with contempt: You *are* a weak fool. One maiden, neither especially lovely nor wise, has broken your spirit with ease. You were too cowardly to take her and you were too cowardly to spurn her—for you feared losing those tiny, fleeting signs of her favor and affection that she tossed over to you now and then, like cake crumbs tossed to a pliant little bird to keep it from flying away.

But now she is gone. And your great test is upon you. You and Pawel cannot both be my beloved. Either you will overcome him or he will overcome you.

I was shocked at her words. Pawel was not only my dear and close friend, but he was also her devoted acolyte. It was Pawel, after all, who had searched for her and freed her after centuries of captivity buried in that mound in the woods. How could she now turn upon him so cruelly?

But when I raised these objections on my friend's behalf, she answered that the one worthy of her love and her gifts would be strong enough to break free from the tyranny of shame and guilt, wherever those poisonous weeds sank their roots into his soul.

And then she returned to her box.

I sat there alone, mulling what course of action to take. But the more I pondered this matter, the more obvious the answer became: I must kill Pawel. It was one thing to take a pig from a peasant. But to assert my dominion, my will, over the life of my closest friend and companion, as if he were merely a cow in my yard—that would merit the love of the goddess. Otherwise, Pawel would continue to take what I desired and slowly vanquish me. He would make me his sniveling, quaking vassal.

I had my servants drug Pawel and then bind him with iron fetters in the cellar. When he awoke, I was there, standing above him. I ordered my dogs to attack him. They pounced at once and their long sharp teeth sank deeply into his thighs and his ribs, into his kidneys and liver, before they worked their way up to his throat and tongue and eyes. He screamed with an unearthly terror and pleaded for mercy.

But I would not yield. To pass the test before me, I knew that I must do this deed and see it through. I did not wish to kill him with a sword or a pistol, as if this were a duel with a fellow nobleman over a point of honor. No, I must assert my dominion—I must kill him like a wild stag in the hunt, like a fat beast roaming my lands whose life I can snuff out whenever it pleases me. Do I hesitate when the stag screams in pain from the bites of my dogs? Then why should Pawel be any different?

After it was over, I summoned her again from the enchanted box. When she emerged, she was more radiantly beautiful than ever before. A soft reddish mist glimmered about her, and I could hear faint murmurs of the loveliest music. She kissed me passionately and said I had at last shown myself to be worthy of her love. Then she said that it was time for me to return to the world. Poland is a hobbled ruin, she told me, and power lies now with the Czar. Take what is yours in St. Petersburg. And then she returned to her box.

As I have been making preparations for my journey, I have realized that I am in need of additional funds to enter St. Petersburg society in the manner appropriate for my rank and ambition. I shall therefore need you, Aryeh Lieb, and your fellow Jews, to provide me with—and then he named an immense figure, I forget what it was, but it was so large I nearly fell over right then and there.

The old *Pan* then continued: I see from your face that you doubt whether such a sum can be raised. You are searching for just the right soothing, subservient words to persuade me to modify my demand—perhaps spread the payments out over time, perhaps reduce them. Who can say in what direction your scheming petty Jewish soul is scurrying in your desperation to keep your dirty fingers on your treasure. But you have now heard from my lips the great power that I wield and how I fed my dear friend Pawel to my dogs. What do you think I might do if a pack of slimy, weaselly little Jews should try to cheat me out of what I desire? There is so much to take—your synagogue, your bathhouse, your library, your cemetery. Or maybe your daughters. But instead, all I seek are your coins. You will deliver the sum I have named in one week to my steward. By then, I will be well on my way to the imperial court at St. Petersburg.

And then the old *Pan*, your father, dismissed me from his presence without giving me a chance to say so much as one word in reply. When I returned to town, I immediately relayed his demand for money to the other Jewish householders. They rent their garments in despair—for how could he expect us to raise such a sum? Still, we all reached far down into our purses, and put off some scheduled repairs to the *mikveh*, and with each person contributing his share, and some help from a neighboring town, we came up with the sum and delivered it into his steward's hands. By then, true to his word, the *Pan* was long gone to his new home in Russia. I never saw him again.

So, Your Honor, that is what I know about your father, the old *Pan*, and his friend Pawel, and the magic box, and the Holy Maiden. I am not sure if all these memories are any use to you, but there it is, what I know.

VIII. The Fall of the New Adam

ARYEH LIEB NOW fell silent. He felt exhausted from talking for so long, especially as his hosts had not bothered to offer him any refreshment—not even one glass of water. He started to feel restless. The light coming into the room through the window had dimmed to a pinkish-purple; it would soon be evening and he should be getting home. But just as he was about to ask permission to leave, Count Alexei, the old *Pan*'s Russian son and heir, spoke again:

You are mistaken, Aryeh Lieb, in thinking your words are of no use to me. What you have revealed to me today illuminates many dark mysteries surrounding my father's death—although not all of them. As I said to you earlier today, my father was a remarkably robust man who was unscathed by the ravages of ageing and disease. He never once so much as coughed or sneezed, so vigorous and resilient was his constitution. Yet, he suddenly died after a very brief illness. This made no sense to me—how could death have snatched him so swiftly, when he was still in the prime of his strength?

The day after the funeral, when our house had finally been emptied of all those tiresome well-wishers, I found my mother weeping in her bedroom. I sat down next to her and took her hand tenderly in mine. But she did not offer any fond reminiscences of my father nor did she express any sorrow at his passing. Rather, she said: It was not there—*she* was not there. I found the room in the cellar, but *she* was not there. Where could it be? Where could *she* be?

I started to ask her to explain the meaning of these strange questions, but before I could get the words past my lips, she stood up and left the room, her gaze floating off to some far distant point. Later that day, she departed for one of her estates faraway in the country. She had left instructions that I was to remain behind, continue with my studies, and make an inventory of my father's possessions in our house in St. Petersburg. As his only son and heir, I should feel free to take for myself whatever items I wished.

I spent the next few days rummaging through my late father's belongings. He had some rings that I fancied, and several finely bound books. There was also some eau de cologne and perhaps a jasmine scent in a small crystal bottle shaped like a green dragon. He had a fine razor, too, quite sharp.

However, when I emptied the closet in his bedroom, I noticed something unusual. There were indented marks forming the outline of a rectangle on the far back wall. After poking at this rectangle for a bit, I found a groove of sorts, and when I angled my pen knife into it just so, a block of wood was loosened sufficiently that it wobbled out and fell down to the floor.

Behind that wooden block was a hollow compartment in which I discovered this notebook with the blue cover that I am holding now in my hands. When I first opened it, I could not make any sense of what was written there. As the text was in Latin letters, and not Cyrillic, I first thought the writing must be French or Latin, but I quickly realized that could not be the case. I wondered if the language was Polish, as my grasp of Polish has always been weak. But when I showed the notebook to a Polish acquaintance, he assured me that, whatever the writing was, it was not Polish.

I asked our servants what languages my father had known, and they all answered the same—Russian, Polish, French, Latin. But the writing was none of those.

And then I recalled that one of my mother's dearest friends had, in his days as an officer, broken the ciphers used by the armies of the enemies of His Imperial Majesty the Czar. When I called upon him, he graciously agreed to help me decipher the notebook.

He sat with me all day studying its markings and symbols. By late afternoon, he had uncovered some intriguing patterns in the placement of the letters. After we ate dinner together, he kept at the notebook until late into the night. Sometime around midnight I fell asleep on a couch watching him work and listening to his alternating exclamations of joy and moans of frustration.

When I awoke the next morning, my noble host was a rumpled, wild-eyed mess—I doubt whether he had slept at all—but he shouted gleefully that he had solved the puzzle. Once he showed me how the cipher worked, the notebook was quite simple to read.

Nevertheless, he cautioned me that the notebook's contents were raving, lunatic nonsense. He asked me if I had actually found it among my father's effects as it seemed so unlike anything he would ever have written or said.

I mumbled something in reply about my father being a private man, thanked him for his help, and took my leave. When I returned home, armed now with the key to the cipher, I dived into the notebook. It seemed to be a diary of sorts, but it did not record the events of his daily life or much in the way of anything that corresponded to recognizable, everyday reality. There were often long gaps between the dates of the entries. He wrote of strange things that made no sense to me: of a Jewish heretic and sorcerer named Jacob Frank and his wisdom and teachings; of the Holy Maiden (sometimes called the Matronita) who had redeemed him from bondage and given unto him dominion over the Earth; of a beautiful woman with magical powers trapped inside a box whom he could summon at will; and of a group of believers who also followed these teachings and met in secret—a group of men who hailed from the highest ranks of society and were desperate for the blessings of youth, beauty, and wealth that the woman in the box could bestow upon them, like some kind of devil or fairy. But these men were never properly named and I could not determine their true identities from the cryptic pseudonyms that the notebook employed.

Although I found this all to be baffling, I read on, hoping to discern what my father's relations had been with this occult brotherhood. He wrote repeatedly and vaguely of dark and unmentionable acts that the lady of the enchanted box demanded from her faithful to show that they had indeed broken free from the chains of this world of guilt, shame, and death. There were obscure references to victims and screams and violated maidens and corpses submerged deep beneath the waters of the Neva.

In the later entries, though, my father wrote that he had somehow offended or angered her. He had flinched before some gruesome trial—had failed to show sufficient fortitude and faith, had fallen prey to shame and guilt—the writing was quite vague. But clearly, something had gone terribly wrong, and he despaired of ever regaining her divine, enchanted favor. He wrote ominous, but terse, notes of fear that her great blessings and gifts would soon be taken away from him.

And then, in the very last set of entries, my father abruptly shifted topics. He now focused upon my mother. She had recently, and inexplicably, become quite suspicious of his activities. She demanded to know where he went at night, whom he saw, what he did, and why he visited a locked room in the far back of the cellar to which he possessed the only key. He had always led her to believe that he was out visiting the beds of his mistresses (and sometimes this was true), and he had been relieved when she had sought revenge by taking her own lovers. But for some reason he could not discern, she had suddenly taken a renewed interest in his comings and goings, and he was certain that she had dispatched men to spy upon him at night.

My father recounted that one morning, when he returned home at dawn, exhausted and still despairing from the loss of the enchanted lady's favor, my mother glared at him with a ferocious rage in her eyes. He had never before seen her look at him this way—her everyday romantic jealousies were merely an impatient sigh and a caustic remark, but she now looked to my father as if she were braying for his blood. She started to say something to him, but then stopped abruptly and stormed off.

He worried that her spies had uncovered what he called his many and terrible secret crimes, although he did not specify what they were. He visited the box again later that day and attempted to summon the beautiful woman from it to come to his aid in this matter, but she would not emerge to hear his entreaty.

Unable to avail himself of the magical lady's supernatural assistance, my father considered whether he should flee from our house. But then he reflected that he could not be sure what my mother had learned or thought she had learned, and a precipitous departure would only confirm her worst fears. He needed first to figure out why she was so agitated and only then he could settle upon the correct, prudent course of action.

After a brief gap in time, the last entries described the onset of his strange, final illness. Blessed by the lady of the magic box, he had not been ill for many years. He suspected he was the victim of poison, no doubt, in his mind, administered by his embittered, enraged wife. He resolved that, once he was healthy again, he would leave our house and never again sleep under the same roof with my mother.

After that, there were no further entries.

I was not sure what to make of this secret diary. I was tempted to write to my mother, but, as I did not wish to accuse her of murdering her husband, I decided against it and instead focused my energies on investigating whether any of the diary's bizarre ramblings could be true. I possessed two pieces of information from the notebook that I could readily verify—the locked room in the cellar and the strange box (which the diary had described in various entries).

When I descended into the cellar of our house, I found barrels of wine and liquor, crates storing various foodstuffs, old pieces of furniture, chests full of moth-eaten clothes, and a vicious cat that had grown fat feasting upon the mice scurrying about the cold stone floor. I was about to give up on my search, when I noticed something odd in a far corner behind a pile of crates—a thick metal door—its lock appeared to have been violently broken open and was now swinging from a hinge.

Behind this broken door I came upon a small, windowless room that housed some sort of crude wooden altar. The walls had been marked with strange symbols, or maybe they were letters of some kind. But either way, I could not understand their meaning.

And then I noticed a detail that I had initially overlooked: On the altar, there were strands of a woman's hair, thick, golden, and fresh, undecayed—as if the goddess Venus herself had left a token of her love for someone in that dank spot. While there was no sign of the magic box, the hairs matched the diary's description of the thick golden locks on the enchanted lady's head.

I reasoned that this was likely the cellar room mentioned in the diary. My mother must have discovered it and had the lock broken. Now her cryptic words to me after the funeral made sense: She had been searching for the magic box and had broken into this private devotional room kept by my father, but had not found it.

I searched everywhere else in the house, but I could find no box that matched the descriptions in the diary. After a day wasted in this futile exercise, I decided to reread the diary to see if there were any further clues that I might have missed. It was during this second, closer examination that I learned, through careful analysis of certain difficult passages and partially blotted out marginal notes, that my father had originally found this box buried in the forest on his estate in Poland. He mentioned two names in connection with the unearthing of this marvelous relic—a Pawel and an Aryeh Lieb.

I thus resolved to visit my father's ancestral estate in Poland. When I arrived, my steward informed me that there is no man named Pawel residing in this district. Well, there is a Pawel who works the fields and keeps some goats a few miles away, but I highly doubt that my father would have confided his most terrible secrets to a serf reeking of goat piss.

But, my steward continued, there is an old Jew who lives in the market town named Aryeh Lieb. In his younger years, this Aryeh Lieb had been a timber merchant who had leased the rights to harvest the lumber from my father's forests.

And now, Aryeh Lieb, you have revealed much that I have longed to know. I am determined to find this box and to summon its enchanted lady. She alone can reveal what else I long to learn. She may also, perhaps, see fit to grace me with my father's strength and beauty—although I am not sure if I am willing to pay her price. Maybe she can be bargained down? But for now, Aryeh Lieb, you may return to your home and enjoy whatever pleasures are left to you in your old age.

With that, Count Alexei stood up from his chair, stretched and yawned, and left the room humming softly to himself. In the fading twilight, Aryeh Lieb turned to the young steward, who appeared sad and downcast, or maybe just exhausted from such a long day of translating between French and Yiddish. The young steward motioned for Aryeh Lieb to follow him out.

As they were walking back to the veranda in front of the manor house, Aryeh Lieb offered a silent prayer to the Holy One, Blessed be He, to keep *goyische* lords and their dark sorceries far away from him and his family and his *shtetl*. May he be granted the blessing of a quiet, restful old age and a peaceful death in the arms of his plump, wrinkled Miriam.

Other Books by Barak Bassman

Elegy of the Minotaur
Repentance: A Tale of Demons in Old Jewish Poland
King Solomon and Ashmedai: A Wisdom Tale
The Twilight of the Magical Siren: A Tale of Late Antiquity
The Leper Princess and The Court Jew
The Last Confession of Joseph della Reina
The Gifts of the Fairy Melusine
Necromancy of the Demon Maiden: A Gothic Tale of Podolia
The Death of the Wizard Merlin
The Vampire and The Wandering Jew
The Emissary from Mezeritch: A Dark Hasidic Tale
The Beheading Game: An Arthurian Tale
The Holy Sinner: A Gothic Tale of the Baal Shem Tov
The Abduction of Queen Guinevere
The Cruelty of the Fisher King: A Tale of Perceval and the Holy Grail
The Baal Shem Tov and the Heretic: A Sabbatean Tale.
The Starvation Dybbuk: A Cruel Tale of Love and Exorcism
The Twisted Path of the Hidden Saint: An Occult Tale of the Baal Shem Tov

About the Author

Barak A. Bassman received a B.A. in Classics from Grinnell College and a law degree from the New York University School of Law. He practices law in Philadelphia, Pennsylvania, and lives in the Philadelphia suburbs with his wife and two children. He is the author of, among other works, *Repentance: A Tale of Demons in Old Jewish Poland, King Solomon and Ashmedai: A Wisdom Tale, Necromancy of the Demon Maiden: A Gothic Tale of Podolia, The Vampire and the Wandering Jew, The Emissary from Mezeritch: A Dark Hasidic Tale, The Holy Sinner: A Gothic Tale of the Baal Shem Tov, The Baal Shem Tov and the Heretic: A Sabbatean Tale, The Starvation Dybbuk: A Cruel Tale of Love and Exorcism,* and *The Twisted Path of the Hidden Saint: An Occult Tale of the Baal Shem Tov.*